25,000 SEEDS

Where LVE Grows

A Novel

Helen Noble

BALBOA.
PRESS

A DIVISION OF HAY HOUSE

ISBN: 978-1-4525-4860-9 (sc)
ISBN: 978-1-4525-4859-3 (e)
ISBN: 978-1-4525-4861-6 (hc)

Library of Congress Control Number: 2012904448

Balboa Press books may be ordered through booksellers or by contacting:

Balboa Press
A Division of Hay House
1663 Liberty Drive
Bloomington, IN 47403
www.balboapress.com
1-(877) 407-4847

Because of the dynamic nature of the Internet, any web addresses or links contained in this book may have changed since publication and may no longer be valid. The views expressed in this work are solely those of the author and do not necessarily reflect the views of the publisher, and the publisher hereby disclaims any responsibility for them.

The author of this book does not dispense medical advice or prescribe the use of any technique as a form of treatment for physical, emotional, or medical problems without the advice of a physician, either directly or indirectly. The intent of the author is only to offer information of a general nature to help you in your quest for emotional and spiritual well-being. In the event you use any of the information in this book for yourself, which is your constitutional right, the author and the publisher assume no responsibility for your actions.

Any people depicted in stock imagery provided by Thinkstock are models, and such images are being used for illustrative purposes only.
Certain stock imagery © Thinkstock.

Printed in the United States of America

Balboa Press rev. date:5/21/2012

For Erica and Shawn

To go with the drift of things,
To yield with a grace to reason,
To Bow and accept the End,
Of a Love or of a Season.

Robert Frost

Prologue

Driving to her meeting Norma rehearsed what she was going to say. She had become very unpopular since being elected to the school board and today's meeting was going to ruffle feathers. She couldn't help herself as she let out a faint giggle even in her grim mood, as she passed Haupt's Farms; who sold without a doubt, the best fresh eggs in the county. "We have to stop doing things the way we have always done them in the past. We need to hire help from outside. We need fresh eyes to look at our problem -- someone to see the way to a solution."

Norma carried her stress in her neck and shoulders and tried to stretch them out. Nothing she tried worked and she had been in pain for days. She took personally the welfare of children in Salinger. The town desperately needed help, but no one knew where to begin. That's when days before, the clear image of a woman, she had met several years ago had popped into her mind, and an idea came to her. She would call Claire Patterson, with whom she had so briefly spoken at an education conference six or seven years earlier. Surprising herself, Norma couldn't believe she remembered her name. She had heard the speaker while attending a conference in

Chicago and was drawn to go up and meet her. They talked for awhile and exchanged business cards. For some reason unknown to Norma, she had kept that card. Every now and then as she was cleaning out her worn-out rolodex, she would come across the card and always chose to hang on to it, stuffing it back for safe keeping.

Chapter One

Norma was sure she knew what she needed to do. She was looking for the money with which to hire a consultant who could come in to create a new program, know how to fund it, write a grant for the funding requirements, find an off-site location, and supply the building criteria. In the meeting she spoke openly to the board.

"The public school has been hit hard with cutbacks the likes of which we have never seen before. There are no funds available in next year's school budget with which to fund the before-school or after-school child care programs. There isn't enough money to keep the lights on during program hours, let alone pay the staff." Had the board seen this coming? Yes! Had they addressed the problem which had been growing for the past three years? No! As every area in the curriculum was pared back from year to year, they shifted funds around in school budgets, making it appear as though there was enough to go around and deferring fiscal responsibility year after year. Unable to continue this approach any longer, the emergency meeting was called to solve the dire problem in which Salinger now found itself. She continued, "Without a stimulus, the town could lose an essential segment of its future growth -- young families. Our schools are one of the most important elements that keep this town viable and a proud, family-oriented community."

As rural towns shrank and families moved closer to jobs, education and child care were aspects of a family's quality of life which determined if, or where, these families might relocate to. Farming families were shrinking, and even in rural America there wasn't always alternative safe and educational childcare. Not that most of these parents necessarily always thought that way, but Norma did. She wanted more for the children of Salinger.

As soon as she realized the before and after-school child care would not be able to continue, she immediately thought of Claire Patterson. She seemed like someone who could provide the solution to their problem. That is, if the number on the business card was still in service. Before she picked up the phone to call, Norma had needed to find out how much the town could afford to pay a consultant. Embarrassed, yet desperate, and not knowing quite what to say, she called Claire anyway.

Back from the beach after an early morning walk, Claire was sitting by the pool having breakfast and going through her mail. It was the last day of March and there was a tropical breeze coming off the ocean with just enough haze in the sky to make it a balmy eighty-three degree day, rather than a ninety degree scorcher. Palm Beach was a unique place; the snowbirds left just before Easter, and traffic thinned out, yet you could feel nothing was slowing down. Restaurant and retail shop owners caught their breath as they were quickly preparing for a second wave to arrive. As long as the dollar remained weak, European and South American tourists would begin arriving right after the first of May.

Claire loved her life but had recently been feeling restless inside. She was craving a change of scenery -- something different. This feeling was new to her and she didn't like it. It didn't conform to the nice organized life she had built around herself. *Surely this is temporary*, she thought. Far too distracted these days she promised herself she was going to slow down her work schedule. She had good people working for her after all, and she did not have to personally be involved on every project. So far though, morning coffee on the lanai and occasional walks on the beach were as close as she had come to bringing some needed balance into her life. *I'm working on it!* She thought as she considered, *Where could I go? What could I try that's different?* Something different didn't mean another trip to Paris or London. And she didn't want to take another cycling trip like the one through Tuscany. *No, none of these feel right.*

Excited, she was looking forward to next week. She was going to see her children. It was always a highlight -- and one that took thoughtful planning. This time of year they came down from Chicago and New York. This had become their annual family reunion. Claire, her children, and their significant others gathered every April. Right after her divorce, Claire knew she had to find a way to keep the children coming together and maintaining their foursome as a family. So what started out as spring break in Palm Beach evolved over twelve years into the annual family reunion. This April the twins, Ethan and Kate, were turning thirty. Her other daughter, Ali, was twenty-eight. Their family motto became, "Any excuse for a celebration!" Every year they each had to contribute reasons for celebration to the party. Of course, this year it would be the twins' thirtieth birthday. Also, Ali had recently gotten engaged and Sam, her fiancé, was coming with her. For Claire, this summer marked the opening of the thirty-second franchise of her after-school Children's Centers.

Now that the kids were grown and establishing their own lives and careers, this had become the only time during the year when they all took their vacations together and caught up with one another. It reminded her of Christmases when the children were growing up. During these reunion trips they always fell back into being who they were at ages eight or ten. She thought, *How they digress when they're here, and how I love it!* The four of them were very close, and, while the children were growing up, Claire had a saying that they all took to heart. "If you would pick yourself to be your best friend, you've succeeded. If you talk to yourself like you would want to be spoken to, you're at peace. And if you can feel the warmth of the sunlight when you look up, you're grounded." Now, with their big lives ahead of them, she didn't worry about them anymore, other than the usual motherly angst. She had faith they had grown up to understand a deeper sense of their inner selves. She was always there to talk, giving them a place to vent, laugh, or cry. She was grateful knowing the divorce, and the subsequent years, had not changed any of their closeness.

Watching as three egrets lunged across the yard, her focus shifted. *What to do this summer -- Something out of the usual.* She drifted far away, off in a daydream.

Startled, she found herself on a faraway island somewhere, listening to the familiar sound of steel drums ringing. Steel drums ringing? Ringing! It was the ring of her phone. Back to reality she answered the call, though not recognizing the area code. A Norma Nagel quickly jolted Claire back to reality and was reminding her that they had spoken six years before at an education conference. Then, she began describing how her community needed help. Claire remembered that conference in Chicago. It was where she had given a call for education reform. *Those were exciting times*. She thought. At the time, she had just returned from Washington after having been invited to testify before congress about setting a national standard for elementary after-school child care. Since then, the results had been adopted in twenty-eight states (and still growing) as "The Safe Schools Off-Campus Program." The program which Claire advocated confirmed that students, who at a young age (kindergarten through the sixth grade) had the care and nurturing of well-instituted educational and creative programs, had greater odds of graduating from high school, staying out of trouble, and going on to college. The young student model was one of her passions. With the cost of education rising, and important areas of curriculum such as art and music being cut from school budgets, the creative arts became central to her school program's mission. Claire felt a big part of reaching a child's innate, unbounded love and creativity were being dampened. Up until then, the "Off-Campus" model had been strictly a private education program which she had created fourteen years earlier when she opened her first after-school "Off-Campus for Kids" Children's Center in Chicago.

That conference where she and Norma first met launched her non-profit school concept by bringing school systems together with their local business communities. She had worked hard to help those less fortunate have an after-school experience nearly parallel to that of her private-school students. The Chicago meeting had been a turning point for Claire and everything about that day immediately came into focus. "Oh yes, I remember, you came with other members of a group from Ohio." On the other end of the line, she could tell Norma sounded surprised Claire even remembered her group. They talked briefly.

After hanging up both women sat perfectly still for a time. They were both amazed -- shocked really -- at how quickly they had agreed to work together. Claire laughed. The compensation on this consulting project was the lowest fee she had ever taken; the number was downright insane! The amount they could afford to pay and she accepted, was three thousand five hundred dollars. Her standard fee was significantly greater which included a retainer and an hourly rate plus expenses. There was a formula, and it was a fair formula for everyone. That figure assured there would be adequate funds to support staffing, legal work, fundraising initiatives, and travel expenses.

After congress incorporated some of her recommendations, Claire expanded her model to include a non-profit "Safe Schools Off-Campus Program." When school districts in the states which had approved the model learned of this program, she began consulting even though the money was far better when she sold a franchise private school. The "Off-Campus Program" provided a safe haven for elementary school children to learn and develop. By helping school districts maintain a high level of education through the after-school program, children were exposed to things they could not experience at home or, often, at school. Many of the areas which desperately needed these facilities tended to be either inner city school districts or smaller, sparsely populated townships, many experiencing weak economic conditions. There was no doubt in her mind that this would be the case here. Claire opted to spend as few days as possible in the undesirable locales and couldn't wait to return home to take her walks on the beach, attend charity events and the latest art exhibits with friends, or do a little shopping on Worth Avenue. She had grown accustomed to this lifestyle. Although she had to travel often, and spent extended stays at the Children's Center she was working on at the time, she tried to spend as little time away as possible.

Chapter Two

A few days later Norma called back with what she apparently thought was great news. She said she had found Claire a place to stay, a house, which she could rent for three hundred dollars a month. "Norma, that sounds too good to be true." Claire panicked at the thought of living out in the middle of farm country. She tried to bow out gracefully. *What am I getting myself into?* Norma absolutely insisted that she not worry. It was the gatehouse to a farm which was located just outside of town.

Claire had been thinking more along the lines of finding a suitable apartment in Columbus and setting up a commute between Indianapolis, Indiana and Salinger. Working on a franchise school in Indianapolis made the decision to take this project in Ohio easy for Claire. She had heard Columbus had a great downtown, did her research, and was actually looking forward to renting a place in the Short North area. That would be something different this summer, and seemed like it would be the safer option. However, Norma was adamant that this was the solution and that Claire would find the little house quite adequate. While she and Norma talked, Claire "mapquested" Salinger to Indianapolis. As suspected, they were close enough, less than two hundred and fifty miles apart -- an easy three-and-a-half hour drive. *This could work out!* She optimistically thought, as they continued their conversation. "Ok, thank you, I'll take the house." Considering what other options she had, she decided to trust Norma's house hunting skills knowing she had the best of intentions.

The logistics with the Ohio project were an exciting challenge. It appeared the place to live might be solved. Now she needed to get up there and get settled in as quickly as possible so she could get the ball rolling on the assignment. It was already the middle of April. The town needed to fund, staff, and build a new school by Labor Day. Since February Claire had been flying back and forth to Indianapolis and the franchise private school there was due to open during the summer. This time she would drive up, wanting her car there so she could work both projects and complete them by the end of the summer.

Claire checked the weather up in Ohio and packed every warm article of clothing she owned, as well as some summer things. Thinking this through, Stella McCartney and Burberry may not have been the right wardrobe but that's what filled her closets. Living in Chicago, Claire had developed a taste for designer clothes and accessories, and she liked wearing beautiful jewelry. She had an attractive figure, was 5'6" tall, had shoulder length brown hair, and kept a year round tan.

She packed sweaters, a couple of blazers, slacks, several blouses, a quilted jacket, several tee-shirts, jeans, and a couple of sundresses. She knew she would only need a dozen pairs of shoes and sandals to get her through the summer. Her only new purchase was a pair of tall green Hunter boots. Ali and Kate, her daughters, insisted they were a must for where she was going. She packed five big boxes with her clothes, the paperwork, and some books -- she always read lots while away; took them to the UPS Store; and shipped them to her new summer address. Driving back, she thought, *this is not what I had in mind when I said I wanted something different for a change! This is me just doing the same thing over and over again. Didn't Einstein say that was the definition of insanity?* Out loud she declared, "I will take time to be good to myself this summer -- not sure how, but I will!" With a little coaxing, the feeling this was the right thing to do suddenly began welling up inside her. *It'll be like an adventure!* It was not just the project to which she was looking forward to now. She was looking forward to driving through the Midwest again. She had not done that since leaving Chicago; really, since the kids were young. She thought about how she and James would drop the kids off at camp in Michigan. From there, they would go straight to Mackinac Island and check in for long romantic weekends. But even before that, she remembered being in the country as a child. She hadn't given this very much thought in a long time.

Thinking about the summer ahead, she supposed she was still a Midwesterner; just one who liked a little glitz and glamour. She was feeling a child-like excitement and caught herself singing the *Green Acres* song over and over again. It was infectious, much like any annoying song you can't stop singing. She had googled Salinger, Ohio, Ellis County, and as suspected it was in the middle of nowhere. It looked to be a mostly agricultural area. Maybe there would be the opportunity to ride a tractor or milk a cow.

When she told friends where she was going, no one showed the same enthusiasm she did. The comment was standard, "Oh, its Ohio -- you'll be bored to death and back to commuting." She explained the Indianapolis project already had her in the area, so logistically, this made sense. Her friends' comments made Claire consider, *Have I swung that far out of balance?* True, she did not need to take this job. As much as she worked, she had cut back the number of projects she personally took on this past year. Shaking it off, she laughed at herself thinking – *living in the small town of Palm Beach, Florida, and living in a small town in rural Ohio were as dissimilar as drinking Dom Perignon from a paper cup would be.*

She had to have her car up there, so recruited David, her best friend, to help her make the two-day drive. Making the trip regularly, he was on his way back up to Chicago anyway. His business was based up there, and he flew back and forth. He let her know that a road trip was not his idea of fun, and she owed him in a big way for this one. They were close friends and had been there for one another for nearly twelve years, so she knew it was nothing that a kiss on the cheek couldn't smooth over. The plan was to drop him off at the airport in Columbus, where he would take a flight the rest of the way to Chicago. For her, it looked as if she still had a nearly two-hour drive to Salinger from there.

Shortly after Claire moved to Palm Beach, she met David Hurst. They lived on the same block and kept seeing each other getting the mail or spending time out on the beach. Soon they began running into one another at restaurants and events. Discovering David was also from Chicago gave them even more to talk about.

On the trip up they inventoried what all of their friends were doing for the summer. Martine was spending three months studying French in Provence. Sandra and Bob Brown were taking six weeks to eat their way through Italy. While her long-time friends Pat and Stephen Harris went back to Chicago (where Claire had an open invitation anytime she wanted), David reiterated she had a standing invitation to visit anytime as well. The drive also gave them time to reminisce. "How did we meet? Remember that day?" Claire asked.

"You mean when I followed you up your walk and rang the doorbell just as you closed the door behind you. I thought you'd be happy to see me, even though I wasn't bringing cupcakes. Instead you fell into my arms crying."

"Thank goodness I didn't scare you away." she replied.

"True I didn't know what I was walking into. I didn't know if you had just gotten test results back with bad news about a health condition, or your dog had been run over by a car. But I knew you needed a friend."

"I had run out of the house, grabbed my mail and was running back in. I had just gotten off the phone with Ali moments before. I felt so guilty leaving my children back in Chicago while I was over a thousand miles away, and their father had just rubbed it in my face one more time. Thank you for being there for me." She squeezed David's hand. Remembering how hard and complicated things became when she first moved away from Chicago, away from what had been home, and where she had raised her children, always flooded back painful memories. She thought she would die that year.

With her contacts and experience, starting her own child care centers or schools was a natural fit. She opened her first one in Chicago; then, although she had no ties to the area, Palm Beach chose Claire to open the next center. She knew the commute wasn't just down the road but couldn't deny herself the opportunity. The first school of her own in Chicago had successfully opened and was about to celebrate its first anniversary, when the opportunity in Florida had come along. She could start a second "Off-Campus For Kids" school just outside Palm Beach, and she felt she had to commit quickly. *Something like this was what dreams were made of*, she thought. *How could this be happening to me?* She quickly took the generous offer and would deal with the logistics and her family later. The twins, Ethan and Kate, were eighteen and leaving for college. Her youngest child, Ali, was a junior in high school. Claire felt as if she was abandoning her children. It was the hardest year of her life. Then suddenly, her husband James asked for a divorce, which came as a complete surprise. James had his own accounting firm and worked long days as a CPA. For the past year, they barely saw each other from one week to the next as he kept assuring her it was all part of his job. Claire kept asking for more time together; instead he had his battery of excuses and became cold and distant.

"I actually thought the opportunity down here would make our marriage stronger; thinking that if we were both involved and looking after our children and our future, we would band together and make it work." she said. "How could I not have seen where this was heading? James insisted on divorcing that spring. It did not matter what I said or tried to do; it was irreconcilable at that point."

The non-profit children's organization with which Claire had been involved while in Chicago, "CoAWS" (The "Coalition With Schools," known better as "the Cause"), received the donation of a parcel of land in the Palm Beach area. It would be a natural write-off for the organization to give it to another children's school project. To make it all as legitimate as possible, Claire paid a mere token for the land. She gave "The CoAWS" a three thousand dollar donation. What it really came down to, the directors all said, was they gave Claire the land as payment for the fifteen generous years she had spent volunteering for them. She saved the organization tens of thousands of dollars annually by overseeing the administrative side of their fund-raising operations. She remembered James often complained she gave away her talents instead of being paid for the good work she performed. She thought, *At the time, who knew these years were spent in earnest preparing to build my own schools?*

Her work was now taking on more importance every day. She felt split in two. How could she feel so rewarded by her work, and the families that she came in contact with daily, yet feel so much guilt with her own family? "The divorce was finalized so quickly." She said, "I was opening the school. Flying back and forth to Chicago, I had just moved into the house a few weeks before. With Pat and Stephen up in Chicago, I had no one in Palm Beach. You walked in on a day when I really needed someone." Claire was driving and looked over quickly with a smile and blew David a kiss.

"You've come a long way since then. And you've been there for me too. What about all my ranting about my parents, about Justin? I'd have to have you killed if we were no longer friends because you know too much!" he remarked.

They were in each other's top five; those people who have loved you, accepted you, would do anything for you, and you for them -- unconditionally. David and Claire, both having had their share of challenges in their lives, were always there for each other without judgments.

She told him she was looking forward to the project, but lately was apprehensive about going there. "I don't think about my real mother very often, and haven't for years, but she's been coming to mind lately. I always think of Marie and Patrick as my parents, but taking this trip up here so close to home, has me a little anxious. I've been thinking a lot about her, David." Changing the tone, Claire described her early childhood. "I can't see her clearly anymore. I've forgotten so much, but I remember she was an amazing woman. She named me after herself. Everyday seemed special with her. It was me and her. My parents divorced before I really knew my biological father, and there wasn't a set visitation schedule. But when he came to town, the three of us would spend the day taking a ride through the country. Or he would take us shopping or to an amusement park somewhere. I just remember we always had fun with him and I couldn't understand why he didn't come back to the house or stay with us. I haven't seen him since her funeral." She continued, "I remember we would dress up, and we'd sew clothes for my dolls. We'd pick blueberries and bake pies. My most cherished memories were of when the hot summers came. We would walk down the road, or ride bikes to our own special place -- a field of tall sunflowers. Somebody planted it there every summer. My mother said they planted it for us, and we'd go back again and again. It was magical." She trailed off, and after a lingering silence asked, "Tell me about your memories?"

"Claire, you've never talked about this." David said, "Now what do you want to know, greatest, or most confusing? Going to camp in the summers, for starters." He then proceeded to make her laugh about all of his family's idiosyncrasies while he and his sister were growing up. Claire knew his sister Leah and had met his parents several times -- so the stories made them laugh that much more.

They went on talking about their lives, business, and how each saw the next five years personally and professionally. David asked, "What are you waiting for? Why not get involved with a man long term?" Lately, he often asked the question, and Claire's answer was always the same. "I haven't met the right one."

All the way up they laughed, talked, and listened to great oldies. Entertaining themselves, they sang along. They knew all the words. By the time she dropped him off in Columbus, he wanted to go along to Salinger to help her get settled. They hugged each other and knew they would talk daily. As she was leaving the Columbus city limits, she called Norma, and they made plans to meet at the house.

The rest of the way, she thought, *Thank goodness for GPS!* Finding her way from Columbus through farm country, passing small town after small town, and then more farmland everywhere, the GPS assured her she was going in the right direction. Everything looked grey, and it all looked alike. As much as she wanted to be the eternal optimist, she was now feeling as if she may have made a terrible mistake coming up here after all. It was Easter weekend, and Easter came the third weekend in April this year. The noise of loud tractors made her turn up the volume of the music. Everywhere the fields and scenery stood drab and barren looking, as if it had not awoken yet from its winter's sleep. The sky was overcast, it was misting, and the high that day was forty-nine degrees. This was hardly the welcome she had expected.

According to the pleasant voice coming from the GPS monitor, Salinger was just ahead. Driving through town, she noticed it was clean. There were lots of Easter bunnies propped up in the yards, and trees were decorated with hanging Easter eggs. The monitor's voice then told her she was three miles from her destination. Norma had been right about that. Next she was alerted to turn right, zero point four miles ahead. Turning into the driveway, almost immediately she came to a stop; there was a car parked in front of her.

Claire did not recognize the short, roundish, blond woman with a big smile walking up to the car, but it was Norma who came out to greet her. She told Claire to follow her into the first driveway on the right, and there she saw a pleasant-enough-looking little house in front of her. Claire stepped out of her bug-spattered BMW and her shoes squished right into the muddy driveway. *Oh, where am I?* she thought. She was sinking into three inches of wet, muddy gravel. Her pants were now splattered with mud and her shoes were a mess! Norma came up and shook her hand hard, not letting go for what seemed a very long time. She told her how happy, truly happy, she was to see her. And told her not to worry about the driveway, as she was sure it would be fixed before the end of next week. The ladies each took a suitcase from the trunk. Norma stepped ahead and opened the door. Claire felt relieved. Yes, the house was adequate. "The house is very nice, thank you."

Claire's boxes were waiting in the hallway, and it smelled as if the furnace had just come on. She also detected a faint smell of fried chicken and mashed potatoes. "I brought some dinner over when I came in to turn on the furnace. It's going down in the thirties tonight." Norma said. She showed Claire around the house, and before saying good-bye they agreed to get together at ten the next morning. There was no time to waste. Tomorrow was Saturday; Norma would be over to show Claire around the area, and to start planning their project.

The house was pleasant enough, and bigger than expected. Entering the front door, the open staircase lead to the second floor, and the hallway opened to a two-story great room. The second floor had two bedrooms and a bath. Being open to the second story the house felt bigger, more spacious, than it probably was. The back of the house faced east, and the eastern wall was all windows. The dining table and hutch faced the eastern exposure, and the kitchen led off the dining area. The door from the garage led into the kitchen. Claire had already pulled her car into the garage. She brought in her muddy shoes to see if they were salvageable and if they would ever look the same again. The house had its own charm -- making her feel welcome. Walking into the kitchen, it appeared well stocked. A surprise, really; it had all the dishes, pots, pans, gadgets, and appliances you could possibly need. It hardly seemed necessary, as Claire didn't cook. There was coffee and tea in the cupboard for the morning, and homemade sweet rolls for breakfast sat next to her dinner. *Norma had been very thoughtful*, she thought, and felt herself calming down and feeling good again. She unpacked for awhile, and then warmed up her dinner. She could not remember when she last ate fried chicken and mashed potatoes. After dinner she returned to unpacking awhile longer, and then got ready for bed. She made a mental note of what she needed to buy -- some grocery staples, flowers, and the things needed in the bathroom, to stock it the way she liked. She wanted to settle in and feel comfortable in the house as soon as possible.

Surprisingly, there really wasn't much missing anywhere. The other bedroom was set up as an office with everything she would need. There was a desk, filing cabinet, office supplies, printer, and wireless modem. There was also a computer all ready to be set up, but Claire preferred hers. She understood that this was set up so well not only to make her comfortable, but as an example of the community working together with the school board. She was happy that someone had good taste. Realizing she was completely exhausted, she left the rest of the boxes downstairs. Filled mostly with books and paperwork, she would organize them tomorrow.

She got ready for bed and wondered whose house this was. Again, she was grateful to them, this time for putting the big fluffy down comforter on the bed. She had gotten into a habit a long time ago of listing five things that were wonderful that day. Five things she was grateful for, before she went to sleep. This ensured that she always fell asleep with a smile and a grateful heart wherever she was. Tonight it was: *thank you for the safe trip, and for David having made the trip with me. Thank you for GPS, this little house, and this warm, down comforter.*

Chapter Three

*T*he sun had come out, and Claire and Norma spent much of Saturday together. Claire requested to drive so she could become familiar with the roads. They drove around to get an overview of the area and identify some of the landmarks, including the grocery store, gas station, and carwash, which was their first stop given the condition of her car after making the long trip.

Norma was completely dedicated to Salinger. As they drove, she told Claire about herself. "I grew up in a small neighboring town, and since I had the opportunity to leave, I did so for a few years. I wanted to see and experience more. My father's sister lived in New York City and insisted to my parents that I come and stay with her and attend Columbia University. I graduated with a degree in education and took a teaching job in the city. My aunt and I traveled to Europe, went to Broadway shows, and attended exhibits at the Met. My life was so busy that I didn't go home to Ohio often. Although I was happy and comfortable with the whole city lifestyle, something was still missing. I came home for a month during the summer after my first year teaching and saw family and old friends again. Seeing them all made me realize how much I had missed them. That summer I also got to know my husband Jeff. I was out with my best friend from high school, her boyfriend, and they set me up with his brother. It was a blind date, and my heart leapt out of skin when I saw Jeff again. He was from Salinger, our rival high school. I knew of him, but we never dated. Now that old friend of mine is one of my sister-in-laws. She married Jeff's brother." Claire watched Norma's expression soften and her eyes light up as she reminisced. *She's still so in love with Jeff and the life she's created here,* Claire thought.

Norma explained, "I couldn't go back to New York after that. I took a teaching job at Salinger High and never regretted a day since making that decision. The following spring Jeff and I were married. Later I went back to graduate school. With that degree, I became the high school principal. I remained in the school system while my three children grew up, and only recently retired from the high school. That's when I was elected to the school board. You'll have the opportunity to meet Jeff and his brother at the planning meeting. They own one of the larger farms in the area. Jeff's also a city council member." She also described how she and Jeff lived on a lake. It was a lifestyle they enjoyed, so there was no reason to go anywhere else. "We have everything right here."

She described how Salinger was a great place to raise a family and she did not want that to change. The town was in transition and hopefully was stabilizing again. The largest employers in the area were agriculture, a regional bakery that private labeled bread for grocery and fast food chains, and a patio furniture manufacturer which, much to the concern of city council, was experimenting with manufacturing in China. She emphasized, "This could devastate the local economy. They are the largest employer in Salinger and city council wants to do everything possible to keep the manufacturing production facility here." Between agriculture and this local light industry, family owned trucking companies were also good employers in the area.

Now the city council and the school board were working together to resolve the school's child care concern. She had convinced them that The Center would have a long-term economic effect on the community.

Claire's turn, she began telling Norma her background and how she began her schools. "I grew up in Chicago and have three children as well, was married for eighteen years, and divorced for twelve. Time sure flies! When I started college I stayed in the area, and went to Northwestern University. I became involved with helping children's causes in the Chicago area, where I spent much of my life growing up. I was, at my core, a crusader for kids, looking at children's education from the view point of a Mom who wanted the best for her own children, not as an educator. Non-profit work and fund-raising to support privately funded programs and opportunities for children, has been a lifelong work of love."

Claire explained that her degree was in psychology, with an emphasis on child psychology, and a minor in business. While her children were growing up and attending elementary school, she modeled and observed how she could integrate learning into daycare to enhance children's creativity. She approached being a parent and educator from a position all her own.

"It isn't how much can we put in front of children that expands their world; instead, it is how we communicate with them, through their innate creative passions. That gives them the confidence to grow and expand. Once these traits are sparked in a young child, the tween and teen flourishes with confidence, and a creative spirit. This further manifests in mathematics, writing skills, and artistic talent." At her schools, children were encouraged to shine, do their very

20

best, and take great pride in their work. Nurturing their self-worth was Claire's fundamental goal.

"As a result, many children around the country are enrolled and spending more of their after-school time at 'Off-Campus for Kids' sites immersed in creative and academic projects. High school students are volunteer tutors at all the Centers, helping the young students with school homework, thus reinforcing the daily classroom lessons. Assisting teachers, the program is used as scaffolding. By working with students in both small groups and individually they become better readers and learn their basic math skills. In elementary education all of the responsibility rests on the teacher as many parents do not work with their children at home. In two-income families parents are often preoccupied or just exhausted by the time they get home from work and put dinner on the table. After that it's time to get children ready for bed. Homework is often neglected and children slide from one grade to the next on hopes of next year being better, of somehow miraculously catching up. I'd love to see not a single child slip by not knowing to read at their appropriate grade level. Right after school, after a snack, homework is completed. Then they are free to use their creativity in music or art -- and all before their young, energetic little bodies become tired from their long days. It instills good habits and improves grades." Claire continued, "The model proved so successful at achieving these goals that "Off-Campus For Kids" continues to expand."

The model was one she had perfected because it was adopted early on by the non-profit she had worked for in Chicago. They had implemented many of her strategies while she volunteered for them. Thus, prior to opening her own concept schools, she had sufficient supporting evidence to confirm her school's strong program credibility was making a difference in young lives.

Anxious to get started on the new project, Claire spent the rest of the weekend unpacking. Monday morning came, and she was on the phone early with her assistant. Lisa Pernell was already getting the paperwork started. Lisa worked from home, full time for Claire. Originally Lisa worked as her part-time administrative assistant while she built her Palm Beach "Off-Campus for Kids" School. Later, as Claire's business grew, Lisa's responsibilities expanded. Administration was done from Claire's home but since she traveled, she wanted Lisa to have the flexibility of working from her own home, and came to Claire's as needed.

Over the years the business had grown from Claire's own schools to include the franchised after-school Children's Centers. Much like any franchise, the concept was in selling a reputation and a proven success model with the systems in place. The franchisee could name their center almost any name they wanted to, but it was the "Patterson Method" lesson plans, and trained, qualified managing directors that were the influencing factor when parents decided to send their children to after-school childcare. The "Patterson Method" insured each new center gained instant credibility within their communities. Endorsed by The National Teacher's Federation, the National School Principals Association, and individual states teaching associations, Claire's teaching method carried a strong reputation and was becoming as recognized in after-school education as Montessori was for preschool.

She owned six of these children's centers; later sold and established thirty-one other franchises around the country. The Indianapolis center would make it thirty-two. She staffed her own "Off-Campus" school centers. Additionally, there was a teacher/managing director training program run through two of the Centers. She also employed two independent contractors who travelled constantly making regular visits to existing locations. They made sure guidelines were strictly enforced and provided training on a regular basis.

The economics of a non-profit childcare center, like the one they were building in Salinger, was different than a franchise school. These schools depended on community and government support. In order to keep schools fully accredited and eligible for government funding, managing directors at these non-profit centers had to complete continuing education credits annually. As more public school systems adopted the "Patterson Method," Claire was positioned to easily grow her continuing ed classes within her own schools.

She was a strong voice and advocate in Washington for children and for safe after-school care. These centers affirmed the significance of that. She always initiated the projects and did the hiring. Then, between Lisa and any one of the directors, Claire could delegate the rest of the project within a couple of months. An "Off-Campus for Kids" or Children's Center required an average of three to six months to organize. Then it was an additional six months to a year after the doors opened to facilitate and oversee the start up of the program. Claire attracted the best talent to manage and run these facilities. Her goal was to make each Center a self-supporting, ongoing enterprise.

With all the systems in place, Monday morning Claire phoned Norma and asked her to call a meeting with anyone whom she could think of as a potential investor in their own town's well-being. Wednesday, Claire was introducing herself to five new people in addition to Norma. This would have to do. Money needed to be raised. Everyone knew Claire's background before the meeting got started, so they got right down to business. She explained, just as farm subsidies were available, there were also monies available for childcare in the form of grants and subsidies for those schools which were designated as part of the "Off-Campus" program and adhered to certain educational guidelines. The facility would be staffed with one paid teacher/managing director, for whom Claire would begin the search. Interviews would commence fairly soon. The support staff, year round, would be junior and senior college co-op students and interns. Also, seniors from the high school who were planning to go into teaching and pedagogy would have the opportunity to work with the children. There were excellent colleges throughout the state of Ohio with education schools. Their students could apply for full-semester internships, and all students would receive college credits.

Next, they covered the building codes, requirements, and accesses. This year the elementary school was not starting classes until after Labor Day. Last winter had been very harsh. Pipes froze and burst the main water line to the school. There had been a lot of damage to the classrooms and equipment. Only temporary repairs were made to the plumbing system at the time, so school was out until September sixth.

That afternoon, Claire got to know her new best friends who were helping to make Salinger's Children's Center a reality. Norma introduced her husband, Jeff, and his brother Mat. They were partners in their family's farming operation. They had one of the largest produce farms in the area and employed many local residents. She also met another farmer, Ben Donohue, who was also a large land owner in the area. Shaking her hand, Ben looked at her and thought, *So this is who moved into the gatehouse.* These men described their commitment to the education and safety for children in Salinger. Franklin Huff, a successful attorney in the region, was happy to support the Center and render pro bono services. Dr. Randy Smith, a pediatrician, told Claire he wanted to give back to the town for providing him and his family a great place to live and practice medicine. These were community leaders and all sat on various boards; each had a huge stake in the community's welfare.

Driving back to the gatehouse she put the top down and turned the heat up, and, as preoccupied as her mind was after the meeting, she could not avoid noticing the subtle smells of the earth and the sunshine warming her cheeks even though it was still cold out. Distracted, she realized that she had not seen or smelled a northern spring in years. And it felt as though she had deprived herself somehow. Spring was hatching out everywhere, and all around her Claire felt the birth of a new season. The countryside was waking up. Crocuses and daffodils looked like they were strewn by hand all over the grass and under trees. The nights were still cold, but the flowers and the flowering trees didn't seem to mind and began to blossom as if to loudly celebrate spring again.

Chapter Four

*T*his place, charming as it appeared, was giving her a headache. She drove for miles every day, not necessarily on purpose. Much of the time she could not retrace the routes she had taken, or ever again find the towns and places she had driven through. She had never before driven country roads. Not trusting the shoulder, she drove right down the middle of the road. Focused on the road ahead, when she did look in the rearview mirror she sometimes saw a big truck or impatient pickup driver practically on top of her. Slowly, she would inch over to her side of the road, praying not to slide into a ditch while they honked their horn and peeled past her leaving her in a trail of dust and exhaust fumes. There were so many country roads, county roads, and township roads. Having no idea where she was most of the time, her GPS wasn't very much good to her. Unless she was going to a specific address or town, she was at the mercy of wherever she found herself. When it began to get dark, she would program 6009 Polling Township Rd. into the device and would feel safe again.

It was daylight-saving time, and the days were getting longer. Claire began getting in her car every afternoon -- just driving, driving anywhere. She didn't dare go for a walk because she knew she would get lost, and no one would know to come looking for her. Some nights the temperature was still dipping into the thirties. She knew the animals would be cold and hungry, and imagined she would never be found. These drives were her best alternative and had to take the place of her walks on the beach. She was missing Palm Beach and missing her friends. Claire missed smelling the salt air, stepping in the water, and hearing the sounds of the ocean. She began thinking that she really hadn't done enough of that and wished she was at home now to go to the beach. When she was there, she used that time to quietly think and strategize. This was harder. Too, she was hungry for a good meal and craving civilization. Making note of this, she would plan a trip to Indianapolis.

She had not anticipated the feelings welling up inside when she was alone. This environment brought back childhood memories. She and David talked at least once a day."I'm upset, I'm feeling sad, and, alright, I'm feeling a little self-pity too. I thought I had reconciled my mother's death a long time ago. Now driving around this area makes it all fresh again; as if I might see her, which is ridiculous!"

At the age of eight Claire was called out of class one day and was taken to her Aunt Marie and Uncle Patrick's home in Chicago. She found out her mother had died in a car accident that afternoon. How life instantly changed that day, she recalled. Suddenly Claire had two younger brothers, Jack and Jason. She had a father again, and yes, a mother too; a mother who was so different from the memories of her real mother. Walking into the third grade at a new school in a big city, was one of the most terrifying experiences she ever remembered.

With time Claire felt loved again. *Thank goodness Marie did not have another daughter,* she often thought, *Things could have been very different.* This way, Claire became the daughter Marie had always wanted and Patrick had his sons. In spite of the heartache as a child, Claire repeatedly mulled over and over if they did really love her, and felt, yes, they did. She came to feel it was not just an obligation for Marie, but that she truly learned to love Claire. Claire loved them all, and loved being part of a big family.

Claire, her mother, and her mother's sister Marie were as different as night and day. At least that was how her adopted mother Marie described it. She never used Claire's real mother's name in a sentence without saying she was the rebel in the family. Claire finally voiced her feelings as she got into her teens. "Would you cut her some slack! You disapproved of her so much, how could you even really have known or loved her? You made up your mind about her years ago, never getting to really know your sister, or giving her a chance."

Her mind shifted back to this place, and she thought about how she hadn't spent any time in the country, in a rural environment since then. *And what do you remember from ages three or four through eight?* Claire quickly knew the answer; her fondest memory always stood out -- *the sunflowers.*

Chapter Five

Thank goodness for a sense of humor! And oh, talk about out of place! she laughed at herself. All around town, wherever Claire went people looked at her as if surprised to see she was still here. Some days she could not wait to leave this place, looking for any excuse to return home even for a day or two. It wasn't necessary though, back at the office Lisa had everything under control and she reported on the house and mail regularly. *I'll just tough this out.* She thought.

She was making great progress on the Center and after three weeks, she even began to relax into the environment. She could become intrigued by the least likely of details she saw or what she heard, or even felt, and was now noticing and enjoying the subtle changes all around her -- changes in the land, in the air, and seasonal changes in the sky. She drove with the top down as often as she could, that is, when it wasn't raining day after day. But when the sun came out it looked all new and greener than she ever remembered. Slowly she was becoming familiar with her surroundings and picked a few landmarks so she could differentiate the area. The east side had the cemetery. West was the dairy farm with that intrusive smell the wind always seemed to blow in her direction. The smell of manure was pervasive in the area and knowing exactly when to start holding her breath was now part of the odd charm of this place. To the south was civilization and roads leading to Columbus. The northern extreme was the reservoir -- the lake where Norma lived.

The whirl of tractor and combine engines was heard constantly -- waking up the soil, poking and prodding the land out of its deep sleep which lasted from November to April. Every day the landscape changed. Planting was going on all over the county. These all surrounding smells, this kind of place, were not-so-new sensations to Claire but had lain dormant for a very long time. When she and her mother would look out over the sunflower field, Mother would say, "Breathe Baby, tell me what you smell and everything you see." They would break down all the smells in the air and describe everything they could see in front of and all around them, looking for the minutest details. Like a bug walking up a corn stalk, a ladybug on a blade of grass, or the rings inside a sunflower, then the seeds beginning to form. Then she would say, "There is so much to notice in the world. Always look around you. See what surrounds you." It left such a powerful impression on Claire she used this exercise while raising her own children, sharpening their senses, and continued using the exercise daily in her schools.

Rumors were spreading. "Looks like Ben Donohue has company this summer. That black BMW convertible you see everywhere, that's her." said Charity.

Claire was constantly seen driving in and out of Ben's driveway. He was a powerful figure in the county and the most eligible bachelor. He was gone all winter long, so people could not keep up with his life. That made him a mystery and fair game for gossip. There were plenty of stories, and not all of them were complementary. Every summer, he returned alone to manage his farm throughout planting season and harvest. Then he would disappear again. This year it looked as though he had a woman staying with him. People talked, and didn't expect she would stay long.

If you were new to Salinger, it usually meant you were coming to work at the hospital or were just passing through. Charity Nagel kept seeing this new woman driving through town. She saw her car parked at the grocery store, the post office, even at the Spanish market. She passed her while driving and often saw her stopped by the side of the road taking pictures of the fields, pastures, and the flowers. Charity would say to friends, "You'd think she's never seen a farm or a tree in her life. She's jumping around all over the county. She's probably here from either Chicago or New York. From the looks of her, she couldn't possibly be nice and look how fancy, except for the green boots. What's with the green boots? They remind me of Daddy's when he worked in the fields when I was growing up." Charity had made up her mind about Claire. She was fair game and provided good gossip material.

Salinger's city limits were three miles from the farm where Claire stayed. She was pleasantly surprised the town had weathered time as well as it had. Named after a wealthy "Easterner" who had made his money manufacturing uniforms and blankets during the Civil War, Henry Salinger settled here with his family after the war in the early 1870's. It had always remained a small rural community never bigger than twelve thousand residents and evened off today at about eight thousand. Like most small farm towns, it was proud but had clearly seen better days and more prosperous times. The image one always formed when driving through small towns throughout America was that of dwindled populations, businesses closed down, and buildings vacated and in disrepair. Many communities sadly looked like ghost towns and had lost their identities. Salinger, however, had survived the changing times. It had its own stoic Midwestern farming character that never went away. Downtown, the main street was Poplar Avenue. An interstate bank sat at one end of the business district, and eight blocks away stood a national bank branch. In the middle of town was the U.S. Post Office, the Spanish grocery store, the liquor store which had replaced the IGA, and Fuhrman's Realty. There were a few vacancies on either side of these businesses, but the pizza shop, dry cleaners, hairdresser, barbershop, food bank, Army Recruitment Office, and small variety stores filled out the business district. There was also DJ's Diner, where the vets all came in for lunch and told war stories just about every day. At the intersection of Poplar and Elm were the public library and the other realtor in town. On the other side of his office were the Bakery Donut Shop and the Discount Dollar Store. All the streets had tree names. And two blocks down from Poplar and Cedar was the park on Maple with the war memorial statue. It was a who's who of heroic deeds. This town had sent its best to serve their country and thankfully most did return home. Here on the statue, still a work in progress, were the names of the men and women who fought and served in two World Wars, Korea, Vietnam, Iraq and Afghanistan. Veteran's Day was as celebrated as the Fourth of July, and all summer long red-white-and-blue garlands draped around the verandas and the front tree of most homes. Many proudly flew their American flag in their yards and on their trucks, honoring their identity.

Further up, Maple Avenue intersected with the truck route, Highway 72. Three car dealers, a few vacant lots, the MiniMart Gas Station, Save Way Market, a now-closed 7-Eleven, The Country Inn Restaurant, and a Chinese take-out restaurant made up much of the shopping along 72. There were a few doctors' offices in town, as well as dentists, and the hospital was at the other end of town on Cherry Way. Several churches dotted the area, and Claire noticed one that resembled the little white church in the movie *Summersby.*

The high school, elementary school, and middle school took up a two block area between Maple and Pine Streets. Claire often drove back and forth through this part of town, looking for what she could be missing and trying to locate where a Center could be built for best access to the elementary school.

Driving through the area, and asking Norma for directions to stores and businesses, Claire discovered if you needed a hardware store or the John Deere dealer, you had to drive thirty-two miles. To buy your children a pair of shoes and school clothes was a forty-five minute drive. Loew's was an hour away, and the closest Wal-Mart was a fifty minute drive. She drove an hour and a half, almost to Columbus, to buy good whole grain breads, olives, wine, fish, and cheese.

Chapter Six

*I*t was getting dark, so Claire returned home and pulled together whatever she found in the fridge. Dinner was a repeat performance of cheese and crackers, a big juicy apple, and a glass of wine. Other than occasional dinners with Norma and Jeff, she was pretty much on her own all the time. She had a trip planned for Indianapolis the early part of next week and looked forward to getting to the city for a few days. It seemed to her she had never driven so much, or spent as much time in a car, as she was doing up here. Feeling a little home sick she reminded herself, *Whatever happened to wanting a change of scenery and experiencing something new!*

Thinking back over these years since building the schools she questioned, *How did I end up alone like this?* Sometimes it felt like she had been married such a long time ago. In retrospect, she had seen all the warning signs long before her marriage actually failed. She just didn't want to recognize them. She wanted to be immature, rather than responsible for herself. How many friends had she "been there for" through their disappointments and sadness? She thought, *Why was it so easy to give good insight and understanding to others yet not always be effective for myself?*

She got into her pajamas early and called David. "We have no life but I'm glad you're there."

"Speak for yourself, I just got back from dinner" he said. They caught up on their day then their conversation turned philosophical.

"It just takes some of us longer to grow up than others. We all need time to grow into our own selves. That takes time, and it takes alone time. Not lonely time, but learning to be happy, by ourselves, with ourselves. Sometimes it is our choice, and other times the choice is made for us. Isn't that what a divorce brings, or a death, or losing a job?"

David said, "Yeah, you get past the hurt or let go of the anger you're feeling about the situation, and be open to new possibilities. It's like being upgraded, only from inside. It's a new way you come to relate to yourself and it changes your point of view on everything."

"I like that, an upgraded version of myself. You become courageous, more self aware, and have more faith in yourself." She said. "Growth can come at different times for different people. For some it's in the beginning, right out of school when taking our first job, if we're alone we make those first decisions in our careers and learn to trust ourselves. Or it could come in the middle, as the aftermath of a divorce or other difficult transition -- who to trust then but ourselves? Or growth could come later, as in the case of a long marriage when one spouse dies and the one left learns to recover their courage and have faith in themselves again."

"And you're right," she added, "Let things go – but getting past the heartbreak and letting go of anger are different than becoming aware or our strengths and trusting ourselves. It's a deeper level of coming to know yourself -- it's harder to let go of things that have happened in the past. We may deceive ourselves into thinking we've overcome the situation.

Like my divorce." Being unhappy for more years than Claire wanted to admit, it was her secret that she felt massive guilt and resentment after the breakup. She emerged from the relationship feeling betrayed, alone, and afraid. She was lonely, even though she was surrounded by people and had a business that kept her focused all day.

"David, I carried it with me for years before I let James go. I kept stuffing the sadness away. There was so much going on in my life I could justify it, but more likely I was hiding from it. I could be the victim and wore that proudly. Sick, right? But then, my heart decided it didn't want to be ignored anymore. It wasn't until I really felt it deep down, until I became aware of the discomfort and consciously decided to finally surrender the feelings, letting them go, that I began to heal. That's when I began to free myself. That's when things started happening. When I finally sat and felt the grief, named how I was feeling, and released those emotions, knowing I couldn't carry them inside me anymore, I began to feel differently, relieved. I didn't resent him anymore. I wished him well and wanted him to be happy; and I meant it. You're right, don't hold on to the past or a situation past its time. You've outgrown it by then. Let go of what you think you still want – for what you're really wanting."

Before they hung up David added, "Yeah, don't be hung up on the little picture think big picture."

As she got ready for bed she thought about her dating experiences over the past few years. *Thank goodness I eventually realized after our break-up every man I dated was James! Although he may have had a different nose, hair color, or height; still, I kept choosing James clones again and again. I even came close to marrying a couple of these clones. No, clowns.* She had proven Einstein's theory yet again. The question finally came to her, *Why would I repeat my life? There's so much more!*

She began dating again but didn't seem to find a deep connection with anyone. First, she discovered what she did not want. Now she knew what she wanted and what was important to her. That raised the bar for the next man who would come into her life. When the right person came along, they would not be just two people doing their own things while taking turns to sacrifice time and energy to do what the other wanted. No, instead she knew, with the right person, the sacrifices would be minimal, and they would each do things that would make the other feel enhanced. *Well, good in theory though tough to put in practice,* she smiled and thought. It just did not seem quite as easy finding that kind of connection this time around.

With a smile, just before turning out the lights, she said, "Thank you for this project, for the flowers blooming all around. Thank you for showing me the births of those calves today. Thank you for opening my eyes more and more to myself, and for friends – for David."

Chapter Seven

*C*harity kept seeing the new woman wherever she went. One day she stood behind her in the grocery store checkout line. Claire turned around and said, "Hi, could you please tell me where I could find a good butcher shop in the area?" All Charity noticed was her warm smile and how her eyes sparkled. Not normally noticing someone this way, she collected herself. "Go to Steiner's Country Market. It's a country style grocery store when you walk in, but at the back is a good butcher shop. The beef and chicken are grain and grass fed." With groceries in hand, Claire thanked her, smiled, and said she would see her again.

The next day was a dreadful one. Charity got into a terrible fight with her sister. On top of that, she forgot to pick her granddaughter up from the babysitter after lunch. She only remembered after her daughter called fuming, saying she didn't care about her own grandchild. Things went from bad to worse as the day wore on. By the time she and Mat were meeting Jeff and Norma for dinner, she was all ready to tell Norma not to expect her vote for re-election to the school board. During the course of the day, Claire kept popping up in Charity's mind. She seemed nice, friendly, and looked, well -- happy.

Charity smirked, *Happy? What planet was she from? When was the last time I used that word? When was the last time I was happy? Well, it was when the children graduated from college. After all, there would be no more college tuitions to pay. Then the grandchildren were born. Three years ago Mat gave me that diamond necklace. The jeweler called it an eternity necklace. I was happy then.* She loved seeing the look on the faces of her friends and family when he gave her the necklace for their twenty-fifth wedding anniversary. She kept it in her jewelry box, knowing she really should wear it more often. Mat often asked why she never wore it. "I do," she replied, "but just on special occasions." *What marked a special occasion? They all came and went -- the weddings, graduations, christenings. It seems like there were plenty of opportunities to wear the necklace.* But in her unhappiness, nothing really felt special at the time. She needed to search her memory; *when else was the last time I was happy?* She stopped abruptly. There was no time to think about this now. It was time to go to dinner. Besides, it only made her feel worse to think about it, and she already had a headache which nothing could take away all day.

She saw Claire again at the grocery store the following week. Surprised Claire even remembered her, they began to talk. "I drove to an Amish auction last weekend. There were quilts, baked goods, furniture, and all kinds of farm equipment being auctioned." Taking their conversation outside to the parking lot Claire introduced herself and they chatted for what seemed a long time. The time flew, and for some reason Claire made Charity feel comfortable. She even felt giddy and happy to be there. Claire didn't make her feel as if she was better than her. When Charity was around people who came from outside of town, she always felt they thought they were better than her. Claire had a warm smile and always laughed as she talked.

Charity had come to live in Salinger after marrying her husband, Mat. He and his four brothers were the best catches in school. Mat was the most athletic and best looking of the brothers. She was from the next town over, and she always told people proudly that the town had a reputation for having girls who were smart and pretty too. She was part of a big family. They lived on a small family farm, and her father had worked as the manager of the John Deere distributor for thirty years. He knew everyone within the tri-county area. When she was a child, she thought he was a town celebrity. It seemed to her every man knew her dad as he shook hands and talked to everyone he saw. She was the youngest of five children. Her parents were now in their eighties, still healthy and active.

She and Mat had met at a football game in high school, falling in love instantly. That year she was a sophomore and he a senior. They both went off to college promising each other to return home after school. Mat came from a large farming family in the area. Nagel Farms was one of the biggest farms in the tri-county. Everyone knew them, and yes, she was marrying a Nagel. She became a teacher but only taught for a year. They started their family immediately. And her family, the community, and their church became the focus of her life. Mat got his degree at Ohio State in horticulture and knew he would eventually run the farm's growing operations. His farm was their future, and he promised her a secure life. Within this industry, he knew he would have a recession-proof career, promising Charity a simple, blissful life without more than the trials of weather and broken-down machinery.

Charity and her sister-in-laws were all active at church, providing plenty of opportunity to see one another and stay caught up on all the family gossip. All but Norma; she was the quiet one who kept everything to herself. She and Norma could barely stand each other. They were both from the same neighboring town of Oakville. They had been best friends, and subsequently rivals, all of their lives. They both married Nagel's and lived just two miles apart. Their husbands demanded they call a truce a long time ago, and now they tolerated one another. Every year the Ellis County Fair was planned for the second weekend in August. Along with Cathy and Barb, their other sister-in-laws, this year they were all on the county fair board committee together. Meetings were held twice a week, and usually much of the time was spent trading gossip about goings-on in town and in the family. Charity thought Miss Snooty, Norma, probably wouldn't stay after for coffee again. Just as well, since she didn't like Norma spoiling it for the rest.

Norma had been calling the house a lot lately needing to talk to Mat, and when Charity asked what it was about, he always replied it was about the school. She believed him, because she knew Norma wasn't his type. Oh, there had been jealousy and fighting in the family before; but she knew that Jeff and Norma kept to themselves as much as they could.

Chapter Eight

$\mathcal{M}$at's farm had been in the family for one hundred and nineteen years. Each generation added to the farm. In these counties, land didn't change hands very often. It simply passed down from generation to generation. The way additional land was acquired occurred when a farmer noticed that another farm in the area was in disrepair or doing poorly. First, the farm buildings would show signs of neglect; then the fields would become overrun with weeds and there would be late or lost harvests. Rumors would tell of families who could not pay their taxes or of a dying farmer. Often sons or daughters came back to farm the land, but they weren't good at it and disliked farming. This gave the other farmers in the county a chance to make an offer to the overwhelmed widow or children, buying the land below market value. This ensured the land, and the town of Salinger, remained in the hands of the local families so no outsiders came in. This practice had worked for a very long time and served the local families well. But things were beginning to change.

More Amish and Mennonites were moving into the area. Ohio Amish country was growing. This area always had a fairly large Mennonite and Amish population. They had their close-knit communities, businesses, schools, and farms, but now they were growing in numbers. Because of them, the price per acre of rich farmland was going up. Local farmers were still looking for bargains while the Amish were driving land values higher.

The Amish and Mennonites were dairy, wheat, and corn farmers. In some instances their families were growing and there was not enough land in Pennsylvania to sustain their growth. They sold their farms in order to buy larger tracks of land elsewhere. Many farmers throughout the counties surrounding Lancaster County, Pennsylvania, were selling their fertile land and they instantly became very wealthy families. Much of this land was then resold to commercial real estate developers. The rich, fertile soil, where you could drop a seed into the ground and it would grow to perfection, was now being covered over. Cinderblock foundations and homes were dug into, and growing up out of the fertile ground. It was a developer's dream. The land had been cleared a long time ago. Homes could be built and sold in record time, creating safe, charming country communities. The commutes were at least an hour or two one way to work, but the sense of security must have seemed worth the drive as neighbors worked in Baltimore, Maryland, Washington D.C., Philadelphia, and Harrisburg, Pennsylvania.

Many Amish and Mennonites left those farms but were, at their core, still farmers who wanted to continue working the land and making a living doing so. They all seemed to have relatives or friends of relatives in Ohio and quickly migrated west. What seemed to the locals as outrageous offers to buy parcels of land sent land values skyrocketing overnight. The Amish and Mennonites were buying farms throughout the area right out from under the likes of the Nagel brothers, and their communities were growing. One had to be very careful driving because there were more and more black Amish buggies taking their time, gently rolling along the roadways. They were building beautiful barns and fences. The more liberal minded of the groups were buying steel wheeled tractors instead of using horses to work the land. And they built themselves spacious lovely farmhouses, with no electricity of course.

Mat's family farm had a succession plan that included sons. Daughters had no claim to the farm even if their husbands could help bolster the business -- there were no exceptions to the rule. When the farm began over one hundred years ago, there were two brothers. During the next generation, the men had one son each. And two generation later came Mat, his brothers, and nine cousins. Mat had four brothers, and now each of them had more sons than daughters. The partners in the farm now numbered twenty-six.

The farm was a jewel in the area, second only to Ben Donohue's. They had seventeen hundred and fifty acres of prime fertile farmland, growing peppers, cucumbers, radishes, zucchini, squash, and miles of acres of corn. But as big and robust as a crop season could be, assuming no interference from Mother Nature, the State Department of Agriculture, U.S. Citizenship and Immigration Services, or OSHA, the partners were growing to be too many in number for the profits to sustain. By the next generation, the farm could see a drop in the ability to sustain the lifestyles to which all of the family members had grown accustomed. They all lived well, yet the millions of dollars which the farm annually generated never seemed enough to give each member of the family his expected share.

By Mat's generation, the farm had become big agriculture. Fertilizers and pesticides had changed the landscape. There was abundance from year to year. Charity remembered always living well. Even when they were first married, they were making so much money selling their produce, it seemed she could plan the house they eventually built and have everything she wanted in the plans. They built a nice four-bedroom home on two acres. She remembered when she and Mat went shopping in Columbus one weekend. They bought and paid for all the furnishing and accessories for the whole house in cash. They stayed overnight that weekend and she had room service for the very first time. That was when they made baby number two, their daughter Jenny. They raised all four of their children in their farmhouse, which looked tired now; as tired as she felt most of the time.

They had one son, Peter. Being the only son made him Mat's only heir to the farm. Peter returned home right after college. He felt the same way many of his cousins did. Most did not dream of farming as their fathers had and made little of the real effort required to run and grow the business.

It was fortunate Peter wanted to stay home, Charity thought, because her sister-in-laws had more sons than she and most of them were part of the farm now. She wasn't happy about it, but it would always be that way.

Of their other children, two of their daughters lived in nearby towns. Jenny was a teacher, married with one child, and her other daughter Pam was a physical therapist right there in Salinger. Their oldest daughter, Melisa, moved to Chicago. She was married and had two children. Charity did not like her son-in-law Brad. Yes, he was a good husband, and her daughter seemed happy. He was a wonderful father, and he had an excellent job doing something in banking. For no particular reason, she just did not like him, and it bothered her that Mat did not agree with her.

Chapter Nine

$\mathcal{T}$hroughout May, as the sun climbed higher in the sky, the flowering trees brightened the landscape, and the grass knew where to grow filling in all the spaces where the earth had sat bare. The flowering plum trees were pastel pink. There was a solid row of flowering pear trees planted up both sides of the driveway which created a billowing white tunnel made of soft almost translucent white petals leading toward the main house in the distance. Claire's best view of the trees was from the dining room window as she sat enjoying her breakfast and morning coffee. In the early morning sunlight and crisp still air, the morning dew glistened everywhere. It illuminated each blade of grass, every contour in the land, and it softly lit up the tree line that graced the long, gently sloped driveway. It looked like an oil painting hanging before her as she sat admiring the exhibit.

Claire made her trip to Indianapolis and returned fully stocked. Her fridge was reminiscent of home back in Palm Beach again. It was stocked with an assortment of dips, crackers, cookies, breads, nuts, olives, fresh herbs, fruits, vegetables, wines, and several of her favorite cheeses. Unfortunately, she discovered quickly that she had to resort to preparing her own meals. Cooking for one was hard anyway, but she also had not cooked in such a long time she was finding it difficult to get motivated to begin again. While in the city, she also bought some new clothes, going for the Target collection this time. And before driving back, she took some extra time to purchase a new camera. What had started as taking snap shots when she first arrived was now turning into something she focused much of her spare time on. Photography was something she always wanted to do but never made a priority. She kept telling David and others about what she was seeing but knew words could barely describe the way it really looked. She was waking up to the beauty around her. That week Claire decided she had to make a choice. *This is a temporary experience, so why not get into it, touch it, and explore it!* She knew the dirt and dust were not going to hurt her and she had to stop wearing clothes which all had to be dry-cleaned. She decided her jewelry ought to be temporarily retired as well.

Excited about her little pep talk, she was camera ready and began taking pictures on the way back to Ohio. The redbuds were springing up all along the roads and in people's yards. They were always one of her favorite trees. The buds tightly wrapped themselves around the branches and always reminded her of little Christmas lights strung up and down the thin branches. She remembered from her Chicago days that, within a couple of weeks, the dogwoods would come in full bloom as would the crabapple trees.

On Monday, she finished up for the day and wanted to get out and see what was new around her. She was pulling out of the driveway while on the phone with Lisa. Hitting the gas, she began pulling out as always -- fast. Suddenly, she heard a loud screech and the skidding of tires on gravel, and a long, loud horn blast. She had pulled out in front of her neighbor's truck while it was coming down the driveway. Through the rearview mirror she saw the truck had swerved to miss her. She slammed on her brakes and came to a screeching stop just in time, barely missing the truck. She had never seen anyone come down that driveway before! Claire quickly jumped out of the car and came around to see a fancy, clean white pickup truck in the ditch along the driveway. It had just missed the trees by inches on one side, and her whole passenger side on the other. She quickly got back in and pulled up so the driver could get out of his truck. She recognized the face. It was Ben Donohue from the Children's Center meeting. Claire could not stop apologizing, and Ben could not wait to get his truck out of the ditch. She pulled back into the driveway and saw Ben drive away.

She had no idea he lived there. She paid the rent to Norma. When she had asked who owned the home, she somehow never got a direct answer. She never saw anyone coming or going from the main house, so she referred to whomever it was as her mystery landlord. She had imagined several picture of what he looked like, one time he was old, toothless, and weathered. The next, he was brawny and tan. *No, that might be me getting cowboys and farmers mixed up.* She thought. She never ventured up the driveway because she heard a dog barking up there, and it sounded like a big dog. She did not want to be the intruder who made the front page of the local newspaper. After the chaos subsided, she felt like a complete fool. Here she was the expert who had come to save the children of Salinger. Besides nearly killing one of her main funding sources, she now also came across as a complete airhead. She felt she had to fix this as soon as possible.

Checking the files, she called the number she had for him. Relieved, she noticed his voice sounded friendlier than it did just an hour before. She asked if she could just briefly stop by later. He said he was on his way home, inviting her to come up an hour later. Deciding to make a huge sacrifice in the name of peace and goodwill, Claire took her recently delivered favorite chocolates from home to give to her neighbor. Luscious Lucy Chocolates were, by far, one of the best peace offerings she could think of.

Driving through the tree canopy she was pleasantly surprised to see the beautiful house in front of her. It was not at all like the farmhouses that could be seen throughout the area. It was very private and could not be seen from any roads. It was immaculately landscaped, surrounded by trees on three sides, and it appeared to look out the back onto a large parcel of farmland. Claire pulled up in front and went to ring the doorbell. Instantly a big excited black dog appeared on the front porch. *I forgot about the dog!*

Ben came to the door and greeted her, "Hello again. Don't worry, Max is friendly. Go on, boy," he said to the dog, and the dog immediately obeyed. "I have been meaning to come down to say hello and see how you're doing in the house. The school meeting just didn't seem like the appropriate time and place to ask."

Claire's response was, "Everything about the house is perfect. I didn't expect the next time we would meet it would be quite like this. My apologies, again," and she handed him the chocolates. "These are for you and your wife. Thank you for renting the house to me. These are also a peace offering for today."

He smiled and said, "Thank you, did you bring these all the way from Palm Beach?"

"No, I ran out and these replacements just arrived," she replied.

"Then I want to share them with you. Can you stay and have a cup of coffee or glass of wine?" he asked.

She quickly responded, "I don't want to intrude." He turned and walked away as if expecting her to follow, "I live here alone. Come on back this way to the kitchen." She followed and noticed the interiors. There was no mistaking it was a man's home. There was no sign of a woman anywhere in the decorating. They sat at the kitchen table and both opted for a glass of wine. He told her he was fifty-seven years old and had been divorced for many years. She had a similar story to tell. They talked about the Center, the town, the farms, and the area. *Hmm*, she thought, *at the meeting he hadn't even tripped my radar and he's taller than I remember. He looks about 6'2" He's very good looking.* Now she noticed how bright blue his eyes were, and she liked his thick salt-and-pepper hair. He had a warm smile and loud, happy laugh. "Your home is beautiful, but I'm a little surprised that it's so different than most of the farmhouses around here," she said.

"I was gone for a long time and when I returned I built a home to my specs. We farm, but first and foremost we're in marketing. That's what my business was while I was gone. There are several people around this area that left after college and have recently returned to have homes here again. I guess we all thought about how happy we were as kids living here."

"You're Ohio expats." She shrugged. "There's definitely something amazing about returning home after being gone a long time. Do you find that a smell triggers a memory, or something you see takes you back to another time?" Claire immediately transported back to laughing and eating apples and Chex cereal while sitting up on the fence and seeing the sunflowers. She'd eat the apple's juicy flesh and put the skin in her mouth to make a big red smile. Then she and her mother would giggle and be silly. These memories kept surfacing and they weren't supposed to. They were fine just where they had been all these years – buried away.

Claire continued about how she was a full-time resident of Florida, and explained how she ended up in Palm Beach. Ben only spent the winters there and told her he was usually back down, preferring the west coast of Florida, after the first of the year.

The sun went down, and it grew dark outside as they continued talking. Claire's stomach began loudly growling as they looked up and noticed it was 8 pm. Ben pulled out leftover roasted chicken and she helped herself in the fridge to make a salad for them. They finished the bottle of wine, had another chocolate or two, and continued talking - surprisingly, they talked as if they had known each other for a long time, not as two strangers who had just met. As Claire was leaving, he stepped in front of her to open the door and brushed against her lightly. They both stopped and looked at each other. They held their gaze, and there was nothing awkward about it. It was time for her to leave. Suddenly shy, they gave each other a stiff hug as if this evening had never happened. "Good night, thanks for dinner. I had a nice time," she said.

"I'll walk you out to your car." he said, as they stepped out into the cool night. With a shiver she got into her car and drove back down to the gatehouse.

Chapter Ten

*C*laire and her team had been working on the project for five weeks, keeping Norma informed of the progress. Norma was relieved she was no longer responsible for any details regarding the Children's Center. The only job Claire did give her was to decide on a name for the new center. The following Monday morning Claire hand delivered her report with five additional copies to Norma. There would be a meeting later in the week to begin implementation of the proposal.

In the meeting, the group realized quickly there were no areas in the project which could be cut -- nothing to speculate over. The whole plan needed to be initiated as soon as possible. The only thing she could not nail down was where the Center would be located. In the meeting she made it perfectly clear that, in order to make the September sixth deadline, now was the time to either begin a build-out of an existing space or begin construction on a new one.

She looked around the room and directly at Ben. They had not gotten together since their driveway incident. She had thought of him often since then, perhaps too often. She could tell they got along well but that was the last time they had spoken. She had recently begun seeing him on his bicycle. He would be out riding alone through the countryside while she was driving somewhere. Claire loved cycling and briefly thought about buying herself another bike up here. Besides not being necessary, since she planned to leave soon, the main reason holding her back was she knew she would get lost as soon as she pulled out of the driveway.

The last thing that needed to be done at the meeting was to have everyone signed off on the work order and proposal. Claire was seated and the rest stood around the table to sign the documents. As she was signing, her full, dark hair fell over her face, brushing the desk. Ben gently moved her hair to the side. Everyone became uncomfortably aware of what he had done. Yes, it was inappropriate! Yes, she was startled! Yes, she found his touch at once electric! And yes, everyone was surprised and looked right at him. He himself realized how inappropriate it was. He had extended his hand and touched her hair! It had been a natural reaction. He excused himself and proceeded to sign the document.

After the meeting, as everyone was leaving, Ben asked if she was free for dinner. Accepting, they took a drive through the country to a little family owned Italian restaurant about a forty minute drive from Salinger. Along the way he pointed out local landmarks, where friends lived, and they talked about the Center and Claire's work. One of the driveways they passed belonged to friends of his, Bill and Yvonne Klaussen. He commented, "You would love their home. They don't live in the area full time, but Bill grew up in Salinger and was my older brother's classmate. Later, in our careers, Bill and I reconnected and did occasional business deals together. I'll call him, and I expect he'll financially support the Center project."

At the restaurant, their conversation was nonstop and very comfortable. Again, they found they had things in common, especially the discovery they both loved to cycle. She told him she had been cycling for years and had taken two cycling trips abroad with friends. Very occasionally, she rode with a group in the West Palm area. Ben told her he had additional bicycles in the garage. "Great then let's get started tomorrow!" he enthusiastically said. While they drove back to the municipal building to get Claire's car, she asked, "A Range Rover, is it out of character for the environment."

"You're stereotyping." He replied, "I've driven one for years. I drive the truck to the farm, but prefer the ride in an SUV."

There was one awkward silence as they were pulling into the parking lot, to which she responded, "Thank you for a great evening. Let's discuss the building plans soon. And Ben, I want you to know that I had a great time tonight."

Claire stepped out of his car. Ben got out and quickly came around to open her car door. They looked deeply into each other's eyes and neither moved. The moonlight lit her hair; he thought, *I hadn't noticed how beautiful she is.*

As he closed her car door, he asked if she would have dinner next weekend. *Of course I would!* Slowly, she said, "I'd like that." Claire followed him home. He drove fast -- seventy, even up to eighty miles per hour! Up and down the windy, slopey, country roads, she stayed right behind him. If there was going to be an accident this may as well be the place. She was feeling exhilarated and her inner passion was resurfacing. As they pulled into the driveway, he rolled down the window, and waved goodnight.

Chapter Eleven

Resumes were arriving daily for the managing director position at the Center, and Claire had begun scheduling interviews. When she looked at her watch, it was already one o'clock. Frustrated, she thought, *Of all days to have a full schedule and not be able to get away!* There were many details which needed to be addressed at the office all that day, but she had been hopeful she could finish up by noon and make a mad dash to Columbus to purchase some biking shorts, shirts, a pair of gloves and new helmet. Not being able to foresee how busy her day would become set her off balance. It was now four o'clock and they were meeting just after five. She had to swallow her pride and quickly pulled together an outfit. *A "misfit" rather than an outfit*, she winced. Then she became instantly aware of what she was doing – *Oh, a little intense aren't we? Breathe, go with the flow.* She was being too hard on herself, and taking herself much too seriously! Realizing this, she took that deep breath, and quickly changed her attitude -- *I'm working on it!* She could catch herself most of the time when she was critical or judgmental. It was mostly of herself, not as much of others. *At least I'm catching it. That's a good thing.* She thought.

During the summer months, Ben drove over to the farm by six every morning, leaving at five in the afternoons. He was the first one there in the mornings, and his foremen stayed to help load the last trucks leaving the packing house in the evenings. Ben's salvation was cycling. He loved the sport, always wishing he had a partner who enjoyed it as much as he did. He liked to get lost in his tunes and pedal hard. Age fifty made him prone to gaining weight, so about five years ago his doctor gave him strict instructions to start exercising more. Discovering his blood pressure and cholesterol were sky high, he had to make a lifestyle change. His father and many of the men in his family had died in their fifties, which was a family trait he did not care to inherit. Someone suggested cycling, and from the first day he was hooked. Springtime meant he could be back on his bike in Ohio again. Checking the tires while getting the bikes ready he thought, *Let's see if she can ride or if that was the wine talking last night.*

They took off and decided to make this a short, nine-mile ride. "I haven't ridden in months so I'd like to take it a little easy today." Claire said.

First round of excuses and stipulations, he thought. They rode down the driveway, making a right turn. He took her all over the immediate area, showing her many of his farms. Then they headed over to Mat and Jeff's farms where he described how they all grew up together, how their grandfathers and fathers built the farms and how the boys grew them from there. Ben noticed Claire kept right up with him and was within earshot all the way. She had surprised him again. The land here was rolling yet she stayed right behind him, never out of breath, and kept asking lots of questions. He was enjoying this ride and the new experience of riding with a partner. He thought, *She doesn't seem like the type to ask questions unless she's interested*. He was happiest when he was back here at the farm, in Ohio, yet knew most people did not find this appealing -- especially not someone that looked like her. "Are you seeing someone back in Palm Beach?"

She wasn't expecting that question. "No."

He went on, "I just expected you would not have stayed single for long."

"I was thinking the same about you," she replied.

It was a comfortable ride for both of them. As they rode, the time and miles seemed to remove any pretense. They simply felt good. Ben had always ridden either by himself or with one or two other cyclists. It was like everything he did in life. It was on his schedule and on his terms. He liked the fact she could maintain his bike pace -- *maybe there is more to this pretty city girl?*

They kept riding and returned to talking about the land. Ben pointed out the major family farms in the area, giving his own anecdotal history of each family. They turned around, backtracking past Nagel Farms and Claire told him that she had met Mat's wife Charity.

On the way back it seemed wherever she looked the farmland was Ben's. She asked, "There?"

"Yes, we've got four kinds of lettuce coming up."

"And there?" she pointed.

"Yes, onions." All the way back to the driveway, and as they were getting off the bikes, she said, "And out there?"

"Yes, three hundred acres of corn." He answered. They put the bikes back in the garage and stood in the driveway. Sunset was ablaze behind the house. Watching the beautiful sunset they stood side by side, aware of each other's bodies standing close. Their arms brushed together slightly from time to time, and they just stood there. When the sun dropped behind the trees in the distance and couldn't be seen anymore, he put his arm around her and gave her a big hug. "Want to do this again tomorrow?"

"Love to!" As she walked to her car, she felt his eyes on her body. She decided she would make her trip to Columbus tomorrow.

Chapter Twelve

$\mathcal{T}$he last time Charity saw Claire they were both shopping at the Drug Mart. Claire asked if she was free for lunch that day. Of course she was free, but suddenly nervous; she quickly declined. What could they possibly have to talk about, anyway? They had nothing in common. Charity was seeing Claire in the usual places, looking forward to seeing her even, yet at the same time trying to dislike this stranger. It seemed to her that, whenever Claire walked in, it was as if someone turned on a light. She had a presence which you wanted to be around. "Alright which day are you free?" Charity squirmed as Claire asked. They made plans to meet the following Wednesday.

Every other Monday she and Mat had dinner with Norma and Jeff. This week, the three who had been at the meetings talked about Claire Patterson and the new Children's Center. They let Charity know it was still not public knowledge, so she would have to keep everything she had heard at dinner confidential. She promised she would and sat there sheepishly. Charity found out that Claire Patterson was important. And she didn't hear anything said about her and Ben Donohue.

It was Wednesday, and Charity walked into the Country Inn Restaurant. Claire was already seated as Charity approached the table and sat down. Sitting next to Claire, she felt out of place even though Claire seemed happy to see her. Charity noticed everyone was looking at them, and she liked that. *Let them talk.* She would tell them all about her new friend later. She would make everybody jealous and her phone would be ringing for days. *Oh darn! I can't do that. I gave Mat, Norma, and Jeff my word.*

Sitting through lunch, Claire listened as Charity talked incessantly during the meal about everyone in the restaurant. Claire did not think she missed a person in the place, and her attention to detail was amusing at first but very quickly turned uncomfortable. She did not like gossip. As she watched Charity talk from the moment she sat down, Claire realized this woman had no idea what she was doing. She did not say a nice thing about anyone there. Claire thought, *She displays none of her name's sake.* Claire was in a good mood, so being an observer was easy that day. As they sat there Claire even noticed a clear resemblance in Charity's face, between her and a classmate Claire had all the way back in the second grade. Fascinated, she watched wondering if this was how the girl would have grown up and looked today. As the ladies parted ways after lunch, Charity asked Claire if they would get together again. Claire admitted she had no idea where Steiner's Country Market was located, so why not drive down together next time.

A few days later, she picked Charity up at home, and they headed to the market. While driving, Claire paid close attention, extracting the directions from the local gossip and personal commentary which poured out of Charity the entire way. Was she making a left on County Road 329 South, or was it at the corner where the man accidentally shot himself cleaning his gun while drunk one night?

Inside the market, Charity introduced Claire to Mrs. Steiner and immediately proceeded to tell Mrs. Steiner, "You are better off without that no good sales clerk Rhonda. She was robbing you blind and a lot of people knew it." She then quickly changed the subject, asking her, "Have you seen Ruth Kramer lately? How does she look? Surely she has to know her husband has a girlfriend in Clayville. He's been seen with her." Charity said she wasn't sure, but thought she too had seen them together. Claire paid Mrs. Steiner for her order, and the two were back in the car. This time, they took another route home; one that was more direct for Claire. The ride was more of the same, and, by the time Claire dropped Charity off, she was on her way home to take a nap. She was completely exhausted and knew Charity had sucked the energy right out of her.

Charity definitely seemed like a loose cannon. Claire was thinking about how many Charitys she had seen and met while working. *What a big liability a town gossip could be to the Children's Center. Hope she hasn't seen me cycling with Ben, a Center board member. This would be a good time to step away from her. Norma can certainly help me find whatever I need from here on.* Yet, there was something in this woman that was calling out to be nurtured, not judged. *Surely her husband, Mat, even Norma have informed her about why I'm here.* Curiously this became almost like an experiment to Claire. Deciding she had the time and patience to see if there was more to Charity, she made up her mind she would be discerning, not allowing anything to interfere with the Center project, but neither would she judge this woman unfairly as wrong or bad.

Charity liked being seen with Claire. She mustered the courage to call and invited Claire to go to Toledo so she could show her where to shop. The following week, Claire picked up Charity again. She liked being seen in Claire's car. It started out as a repeat performance of the other times they were together. Claire became immediately aware of the babble emitting from Charity. *She has so much going for her, yet she lives in a world of negative reality entirely of her own making.* Claire thought as she listened, then interrupted Charity to ask, "How are you feeling today? How are your children? How are your grandchildren? Did you see them last weekend? How is Mat? Did you eat at any other restaurants since I saw you last?"

Charity's abrupt response came as, "How about I'm feeling like hell!"

All Claire wanted to do was to engage the other woman. She noticed Charity did everything to deflect discussion away from herself. It wasn't because she was hiding anything; instead, she had just become one of the walking wounded in a combat zone where she and others who lived in town spread malicious gossip about one another. Claire could no longer listen as it hurt her heart with every encounter. Feeling compassion, Claire could see Charity living on the surface of her life and not engaging with her soul and her senses. She was sure there was a gentle side to her, somewhere. Amusing herself, Claire thought, *She is the wife of a farmer after all! They should be loving people who love the land, nature, God, and their community.* Claire knew she was teetering on her soapbox, understanding we're all human, but it didn't mean we couldn't change if we wanted to. *Goodness knows I'm a work in progress.* She admitted.

Claire kept coming back to her questions and saw the frustration in Charity. As she spoke she jumped from one story to another, always wounding someone. This self-important claim she had upon everyone was robbing her of a life filled with so much more. Every story robbed someone of their dignity. She had never asked Claire why she was here. They didn't have conversations. Claire was game, at least for now, and was determined to start engaging her. Every response had a negative twist to it. Asking her about her daughters entailed stories of how she could never have married the young men they had chosen. There were stories like the one about the woman who lived in the house on Maple Street. As soon as her husband died, the neighbor man went over to console her. Within three weeks, he was living with her and divorcing his wife. Then there was the superintendent of schools in town who was caught having an affair with a minor. Not once, but twice. He was finally dismissed. Additionally, there were the petty judgments, such as that man was a stupid farmer; and rumors, such as those people in the house over there locked their children in the closet. Claire could see, while she was telling these stories, Charity's face took on an anger that did not exist when she wasn't all wrapped up in the drama. When Claire dropped Charity off at home she put the top down. Taking a deep breath, she had to breathe the fresh air to clear the negativity.

Charity went inside, turned on the news, and just sat down. She hadn't been feeling well. She never felt good. If you asked her how she was, she would answer tired, or she had a headache, or was feeling alright that day but her doctor was a quack and couldn't find anything wrong with her. She knew she was about forty pounds overweight but that was OK because everyone was. It was just normal and many of her friends were heavy too. Her daughter Pam never lost weight after having her children. *See, it was just normal,* she thought.

Lately, feeling depressed much of the time she felt no one understood her. She was getting closer to taking the prescription drug her doctor said would make her feel better. He told her there really wasn't an alternative. A lot of her friends were taking Zoloft and Prozac. She had gotten her son, Peter, a prescription when he went off to college. He told her many of the students in his dorm were taking these drugs. They lost their fears and inhibitions, felt more outgoing, functioning better on campus. He wanted to feel that way too, since he often felt out of place.

Wasn't that what Charity was feeling? She didn't like the way she felt or the way she looked. She was mad at Mat so much of the time. He would try to please her but always fell short. And she made sure he knew it. She couldn't quite remember anymore what all these things were about him she didn't like. There were times when she loathed him and, for a long time now, noticed he was just living there with her. Had he given up too? They had sex about once a month, and that was fine with her. She hadn't thought about sex or initiated it in a very long time. That was Mat's department. If he wanted it he could have it. She knew to keep her man she'd better be available when he wanted her.

She assumed he didn't like the way she looked now. *He probably doesn't even look at me. I never liked him looking at me, anyway. It was embarrassing. He used to tell me I was beautiful.* Now he stopped saying much of anything. She thought, *Like everything else that comes to an end, that all had to as well. Isn't that the way it goes?*

Charity could still see the way she looked when they got married. Her dress had been a size eight. She remembered feeling so pretty that day. She was 5'5" tall and wore a beautiful dress she bought while shopping with her sisters. She wore her long blonde hair half up and curled, the way Mat liked it, and wore a short veil. Her hair was still her best feature, and she still wore it long. Looking down she thought. *How can I lose this weight I've tried to lose so many times before?*

For years, she and Mat often fought about her weight. He would tell her to do whatever it took to lose it. She had joined every health club and weight loss center in a sixty mile radius of Salinger. She would drive nearly an hour three times a week to attend. Sometimes she would lose as much as fifteen, once even twenty pounds, but within six months she would gain it all back. She also remembered the trainer who made her so hungry after the workouts she gained eight pounds in three weeks. She stopped going to that gym. She left the kids with her mother and spent much of her week commuting back and forth. So much of her life seemed wrapped up in weight loss, yet everything was an excuse to eat. If she was angry, it was comfort food. If something made her happy, it was a reward. If she was about to start a new diet, or even a new week, she had to eat because it was the last big hurrah before the beginning. Now Mat just kept quiet. He didn't bother about her weight anymore, and that disturbed her because she missed the attention.

She told herself she didn't care. So why was she wishing that things could be different and that all of this could change?

Chapter Thirteen

"This is good." She discovered the Chinese takeout wasn't too bad. They both liked spicy food and Chinese always included a cold beer. Sitting on his patio Claire told Ben about her divorce. She had talked about her kids, friends, the schools, but their marriages hadn't come up before. She said, "I know I got married too young. James and I met in high school. He went to Northwestern University and I followed him there. He stayed, getting his MBA at Kellogg, Northwestern's business graduate school, while I earned an undergrad degree in psychology and business. We got married right after graduation and, within months, were pregnant and starting a family. This was much earlier than either of us had ever planned. It was unexpected but I was happy about it. I wanted a family of my own. I always felt that James somehow blamed me for that though. The marriage lasted eighteen years. I was forty-one when our divorce was finalized." Thinking to herself for a moment, *Even though James was the one having an affair and who broke up the marriage, just because I left to start the school and commuted back and forth actually made some people sympathetic toward him. The truth was he had been seeing that other woman for a couple of years before he asked for the divorce. My schedule just gave him a perfect exit strategy!*

She continued, "As uncomfortable as it was at times, I always stayed at the house when I went back to Chicago. James kept an apartment in the city and would leave when I came back. Somehow, it worked. I think we never could transition our childhood fantasies into real life and real time. He always thought he was missing out on something because we married young. It's funny because he married again quickly and that didn't work out either. He remarried again a couple of years ago and that seems to be working. I'm glad it's working for him." Ben looked at her strangely, "Are you sure about that?"

"Oh yes, I made peace with myself a few years ago, what about you?"

"I won't get married again. I've decided I'm better off by myself," he said. "I got married right out of college as well. I went to Ohio State University. That's where I met and married my wife, Ann. We had two children, Ben Jr. and Sherry. I had every intention of staying close to home. I even gave my word to Ann that we would never live too far away from Ohio. But it just didn't work out that way. After college, I never returned home except to visit -- until I built this house I live in now. We first moved to Texas, then California. I traveled much of the time, and Ann stayed home raising our children. After thirteen years of marriage, she packed up with the kids and told me she was moving back home to Columbus. I was so involved with business I never tried to make the relationship work, never remained close to my children. Paying for their education and a good lifestyle was my way of showing my love to them. I guess, 'Some people just aren't meant to be parents.' I see my children now for holidays, but always feel like an outsider and never feel as if Ben and Sherry really accepted me back in their lives."

Ben continued about his son, "I had hoped, and tried often, to bring Ben Jr. into my business. I intended to teach him the produce business, but we never got along." It probably further damaged the relationship." He supposed. "Yet had I not tried, there would have been the question of why I didn't want my son in the business to contend with." Ben said, "He felt a sense of entitlement and would not accept the concept of working his way up and learning the different skills it took to manage and run a company. Then he told me his mother was right; I was an awful person. Hurt by that, I stepped away except on holidays. It just turned out that way."

She was not touching this one. She wouldn't ask any more questions for now. After a respectable silence between them, Claire got up to leave and said, "It's late. So do we go again tomorrow?"

"See you tomorrow, friend." He said as she drove back down the driveway.

Chapter Fourteen

*R*elaxing on his patio again after riding, he told Claire more about his life. "I grew up on the farm right behind my home." He pointed. "My parents' house where I grew up with two older brothers, was at the opposite end of this 400 acre farm. My father and my two uncles died, like his grandfather, of heart disease in their fifties, and my mom died three years ago. My oldest brother went to Vietnam and was killed in action. My middle brother wanted nothing to do with farming, so he received his degree in civil engineering and moved to Los Angeles. We saw each other more often when I was travelling with my work."

Ben continued, "My father was an industrious farmer, much more so than my uncles. My dad chose to remain independent and never went in partnership with his brothers. He earned a good living and became quite successful on his own, selling his crops to wholesalers and grocery chains between Detroit and Kentucky. That created a rift in the family. Although I grew up with my aunts, uncles and cousins, I left the area for so many years after our fathers died that my cousins and I never became close again. They come to me only when they need to borrow money." He had heard town gossip had it that the cousins and their families resented Ben and that he wouldn't even give their sons, his own relatives, jobs at the farm even though he knew they needed the work. Returning home had its contentious issues.

Claire asked, "But isn't there any way to smooth things out with your cousins?"

"I do try. My brothers and I attended a small Christian elementary school in town, and I believe that start made my life better. So I'm happy to help my cousins, nieces, and nephews send their children to the school. I pay tuitions for others as well; I'm always asking if there are other families in town who need help sending their children. These children I support have to be good students, make good grades, be involved in a sport, and be part of a team."

He paid their tuition grades kindergarten through eighth and increased his support to an additional three new students every year. This took a heavy financial burden off these young families. Some parents worked for Ben at the farm and their loyalty and hard work was gratitude enough for him. Other parents thanked him with home-baked cookies, pies, and flowers from their gardens.

"After college I was gone for thirty years, building a successful produce brokering company that supplied vegetables and produce to markets in the U.S. and Japan. While I worked and traveled throughout the country, I came to know the quality of every acre of land in every part of the country. I knew where the jewels of agriculture were and who owned them."

Ironically, he did not have to look far for the best. Little Salinger, Ohio and its surroundings, had some of the most fertile land in the country. Parts of it were pure topsoil three hundred feet deep. Finding land like this was like drilling for water and hitting oil. It was an abundant natural resource and he knew how to mine it, or in this case, farm it. His grandfather and father had taught him how to farm but he himself understood the business of big agriculture.

"After I sold the business, I always planned to return to Salinger to settle down and be a farmer again. During the last fifteen years of my career, I bought up all the land I could in the area making me the largest landholder in two adjoining counties. I could have moved anywhere, but this is where I feel most at home. I worked closely with my friend Bob Fuhrman who owns a local real estate company."

Bob went to farms as they were about to go on the market and negotiated the purchases. They had been successful at this for a long time, but it was getting harder to buy properties now that the Amish were coming in and placing higher bids for the land. "Bob and I bought land as it became available; then ten years ago I bought into a 2000 acre farm. It was nearly bankrupt so I financed the whole crop for two years, and put all the money back into the farm until it became profitable again. It was a risk, but at the time the stock market wasn't doing well. My money was sitting as cash in the bank and not making any money. In exchange for financing the whole operation, I became an equal partner. My partner died recently, leaving no heirs, so now the whole farm belonged to me. I already had the original four hundred acres that belonged to my family. My older brother wanted nothing to do with the farm, so I bought him out."

Ben owned forty-two hundred acres and leased the majority of his land to other farmers. He also had a few hundred acres set aside the government paid him, as they do so many others, not to farm. He collected a check not to farm around the river that ran through his land. The water remained clean. There was no runoff from the fields of sprays, fertilizers, or farm equipment pollution. When Claire and Ben cycled past the river, she could see it was a nature preserve full of hawks, deer, squirrels, opossums, groundhogs, and foxes. The animals and birds could be seen out in the fields feasting at dawn and again at dusk. There was plenty of food to go around.

This was summertime in Ohio, and, once the plants sprang from the ground, there were workers in the fields all day, every day, repairing or installing underground irrigation systems, laying down plastic, tying up plants, weeding, spraying, and whatever else they were told to do. Then the race was on! Picking at peak, packing, and sending the crates out in trucks, which lined up late in the afternoons and first thing in the morning. Trucks delivered their loads between four and eight the next morning.

Ben's farms supplied fresh vegetables to grocery chains throughout the Midwest, up and down the East Coast, and as far west as New Mexico. The courtships with these chains began long before the first seed was planted. He and other farmers had to give strong assurance they could deliver to both big grocery chains and wholesale operations. Wal-Mart and Target distribution centers gobbled up his fresh produce in mass volume. These pipelines needed to be continuously fed. Wholesalers created long-term relationships with those who could supply consistently good quality produce. In many cases, Ben's father had worked with the family businesses that Ben was now supplying. They knew each others' families well and went to graduations and funerals together. This was an industry where longevity was still possible and where outsourcing was not an option. Negotiations were struck between the time a seedling sprouted and the crop came in. The race to the finish was to make sure every plant planted got sold. Ben explained this was mass merchandising; if they could not produce what the demands were from the distribution channels they had worked so hard to establish, then they would be replaced by a farm or consortium of farmers who could.

Claire had never thought anything about how the produce she bought for her family arrived at the stores. Ben explained, in the perishable produce business, a farmer knew there were only five days from the day he sent his workers into the field to harvest the plants until people bought the produce in the store. The mechanism to make delivery took precise strategic planning and logistics. Day one: The workers cut the crop and brought it into the packing house. The vegetables had to be immediately iced down. The ice room in the packing house was an enormous refrigerator cooler with a conveyer running through it. There the plants were brought to a temperature where they could regain their crispness. Thousands of pounds of lettuce heads needed to be cooled daily and managed perfectly. There is no margin for error. Next, they sprayed a light chemical spray to enhance sustainability. Was it safe? Well, the U.S. Department of Agriculture said it was. Day two: The produce was packaged, boxed, stacked, and readied to be hauled on trucks. Day three: It was loaded and driven to its destination. If it was bound for a distribution center, it was received there to be broken down, rerouted, and shipped either the same day or early the next to your grocer. Day four: Your grocery store put it out in the produce section that evening and the next morning. Day five: You bought it and took it home.

By the time he was finished harvesting the delicate perishable vegetables, Ben's onions and corn were ready for their big showdown. He hired and leased land to other farmers to grow and harvest the corn while he oversaw the onions. Onions were pulled and left in the fields to air-dry in the sunlight before being brought into the packing house where they were stored and kept cool and dry. In the fall, once he harvested this year's crop, he would be filling orders for five months. His harvest looked to be abundant this year, making him very happy.

Keeping a steady work force was one of his biggest challenges and he was the largest farm employer in the county. In the Midwest, with its short growing season, there were very few big farms in the area that required many workers. Those who could, built their own enclaves and brought in their own workers. In some cases, this housing was already sixty and even seventy years old. Ben knew many such farmers throughout the country and they had all been bringing in illegal workers from Mexico for a long time. These workers were brought to the border and transported across by the farmers who planted in both Texas and Mexico. This was a clean and efficient way to bring good workers to their farms. More hands were always needed and a steady stream of workers continually made their own way to the border. They paid for their own passage and shoddy-looking work papers, and then came across onto private farmland. From there, they follow planting seasons; first working in Florida, next in Texas and Arizona, then Georgia, the Carolinas, and up to the Midwest.

This was the cycle and three generations of illegal workers had already worked in Ellis County with no repercussions. And why not? Compared to other farming areas around the country where migrant workers had to pay high rents to live in substandard, unsafe housing developments, here they had a good quality of life. Like other large Midwestern farms, Ben's and Mat's farms had rows of cinderblock cottages -- the workers worked, were paid either minimum wage or by the piece, and they got a clean place to live for free. There was a soccer field close by which collectively the farmers maintained. The workers spent Sundays out there. The other six days they were bussed to where they were needed throughout the day. This went on all season long. These men and women were good hard workers. Their housing here was better than anywhere they had lived back in Mexico. Ben kept his workers close to the farm and out of trouble. Trouble meant deportation and fines to the worker; the farmers had much more at stake.

There are safe havens for illegal workers in various parts of the country. Workers are left alone and employers are not penalized for hiring them. This small Ohio town was such a place. It was not just this town but the whole county that had sanctioned this practice. And if a county or local official wanted to crackdown on the practice, he or she would not be reelected. These farmers made the difference in all elections, and all election coffers, so they got their way.

Ben was good to his workers. He had many problems over the years hiring local residents to do farm labor. It even created a rift within his family because he had not hired certain of his cousins. Alcohol abuse ran in the family. He saw his father, uncles, and cousins struggle with it, and now he watched his cousins' children struggling with the same addiction. Many locals did not take the work seriously. Driving a tractor in straight lines, picking vegetables, or sorting and packing onions were jobs they felt were below them. Ben was determined that, if a man came to work, he had better be ready to work hard while being clean and sober. Yes, it was a known fact Mexican workers were preferred over local boys who came looking for work. Things did get dicey at the farm when he turned away a local resident. He knew he was resented in town and even kept a gun at home in the nightstand. He did not see a way out of the situation.

Chapter Fifteen

Saturday Claire decided to take a trip up to Cleveland on her own. She set a course for the Cleveland Museum of Art. She left early in the morning, making a day of it. She had never been to Cleveland but had heard their art museum was a little national treasure. Not checking the exhibit calendar first, she happened on "The Reigning Monarchy of England," featuring the dishes and serving sets of the royal family. That was interesting, but the real jewel she came upon was Cleveland's permanent art collection. In the mood for the Impressionists she found a great collection of works by Cezanne, Matisse, and van Gogh. They even had one of Monet's *Water Lilies* on exhibit. After leaving the gallery she thought, *I've missed this. It feels so good to be surrounded by art, be in the city, go shopping, and choose a restaurant.* Next, she explored Little Italy. *Didn't every big city have a Little Italy section?* she thought. Just then the smells beckoned her in as she passed by a bakery. The cannolis came in five different filling flavors and the homemade biscotti had just come out of the oven. *Perfect timing*, she thought, as she picked out and bought four dozen biscotti with an assortment of other cookies. These were too good not to share.

Next stop was the mall. She parked by the Barnes and Noble, going in with plenty of time and no expressed purpose. She couldn't remember when she last strolled around a bookstore, preferring to do her shopping online. There was nothing she was looking for in particular, other than wanting to take some more books and a few magazines back with her. The cookbooks caught her attention. But she passed on the cookbook shelves, going up one aisle and down the other, examining all the sections on the second floor. The last aisle led right back to the cookbooks. *I need to photograph food. Cookbook covers are always beautiful!* She was hooked. She had left most of her beloved cookbooks back in Chicago; she used to love to cook. Old friends, James, and the children loved her cooking. For a very long time now, the only time she cooked was when the kids visited. Always fun, afterwards she would question why she didn't do more of it. Picking her favorite three cookbooks out of all the possible choices, she paid for them and couldn't wait to get back on the road. Here was the perfect place to resurrect her talent by making Charity and Ben her unassuming taste testers. She began thinking of all of her favorite dishes. She would have fun cooking again, and this was making her hungry. On her way out of town Claire picked a seafood restaurant. Not readily available in Salinger, every out of town trip included fish this summer. Excited she thought, *Things are going to be different now. I'm getting back into cooking, and can't wait to share the news with David and the rest.* Smiling, she thought, first she had to explain the concept of spending the summer in a farm community in rural Ohio to them; now she was adding cooking to her summer of remaining open to life. *What next?*

It was drawing near dusk. She had just pulled off the interstate. The rest of the way was back roads with about a forty-five mile drive still remaining. She passed a sheep farm. *Not just any sheep farm*, she laughed. Claire kept her camera with her at all times and was happy to have it tonight. The

ewes all had birthed their young and the field was full of
mothers and babies. At least thirty of each dotted the field.
Right at dusk, as the babies were tired after nursing, they
bleated and cried making such a commotion, until settling
down for the night. Acting and sounding like small toddlers
they were tired after a busy lamb day, so exhausted and
ready for bed. The field was filled with little curled-up white
mounds, like cotton ball puffs scattered all over the ground
and large white and tan puffy sheep above them, guarding
over their babies. The mothers would lie down soon, too, just
before dark came down like a curtain.

When the sun went down, it got dark suddenly. This
was scary! Since arriving in Ohio Claire had not driven far
at night. Following Ben home that one night didn't count,
she didn't realize all the animal traffic out at night. She only
hoped no cars would be coming. It was a cloud covered
night, with no visible moon to light the sky. She kept her
high beams on all the way. It seemed as if just then, every
nocturnal animal decided to cross the road. They looked
like scurrying little zombies, becoming instantly mesmerized
by the lights forcing her to slow down. One after the other,
skunks, porcupines, raccoons, and opossums streaked blindly
in front of the car. One or two were even waiting in front of
the garage as she drove up the driveway.

It wasn't too late and she couldn't wait to inventory the
kitchen to see what she needed to stock up on before getting
started. There was nothing worse than being in the middle
of making something and finding out you were missing some
ingredients. And it wasn't as if she could go and borrow a cup
of sugar, or teaspoon of cream of tartar from her neighbor.

There were plenty of pots and pans, some flour and sugar
in the canisters, a few condiments in the fridge, and plenty
of cheese and crackers. She needed to do a major shopping
trip. She would start with the local grocery store for staples

and next trip to Indianapolis or Columbus would include a stop for all the organic spices and specialty ingredients she needed. Sitting down with her cookbooks to make lists, she bookmarked the recipes she wanted to make as soon as possible. Losing herself in cookbook heaven, by the time she looked up it was after midnight.

Ready for bed and sliding under the covers Claire turned out the light. Thank you for a sense-sational day -- seeing the magnificent art collection; smelling the cookies baking, and tasting them still warm; then hearing the gentle baby lambs bleat. For touch, she remembered Ben's arm brush against her skin. Tonight she added a sixth sense -- the sense of feelings. She thought, *How am I feeling right now? I feel content, happy, and tired.* A smile was the last thing she remembered.

Getting an early start Sunday morning Claire had her coffee outside while accessing the yard. She had never planted an actual garden, but contemplated it this morning. She quickly dismissed the whole concept, however. She couldn't imagine going out, tilling the soil, and doing all the things that gardeners do. But she loved pot gardens so it was time to plant her garden on the little deck off the back of the house. She always had great success at her homes, both in Chicago "Pre-D," and in Palm Beach, and loved to see pots of all sizes overflowing with herbs, lush greens, and flowers. She loved the colors of nature's morning haze, like muted greens, soft peaches, and pale yellows, mixed with bold-statement flowers, all coming together. Today was grocery and planting day. She drove to the nearby garden center and bought pots, a shovel, gloves, potting soil, vermiculite, and Miracle Gro. Next she bought her herbs -- basil, thyme, lemon grass, oregano, rosemary, and sage. Wanting to add color, she bought pale green hellebores, purple pansies (her daughter Ali's favorite flower), soft pink, fuchsia, and red impatiens. And to ward off bees, she bought dahlias and honeysuckle. The car smelled like a symphony of fragrant herbs. *Luscious,* she thought, reminding her to stop at the grocery store.

Working on the garden all day was a labor of love. Turning up the music, she opened the windows so it could be heard outside. Peacefully lost in thought, she dug, patted, and watered all afternoon. She somehow found herself feeling content again in this small Ohio town. Ben rode down the driveway on his way to take a late afternoon ride and heard the music coming from the back. There was just Claire's car in the driveway, so he went up and rang the doorbell. No answer. He called out her name several times, so as not to scare her as he came around the corner to the back of the house. Walking around back, he saw her standing there in a dirty tee- shirt with a dirt-smudged face. He had never seen her with her hair messy and swept back. Enchanted, he caught himself staring at how different she looked, thinking how beautiful she was. Sensing his attention, Claire quickly became self-conscious. "I'm finished, just cleaning up and putting the final touches on where all the pots should go. What do you think?"

"I think you're missing something," he said. "I'll be right back." Ben pedaled back up the driveway to his house. Picking out a bottle of one of his favorite wines, *This is a little extravagant, but so what*, he thought as he stuffed a Far Niente cabernet sauvignon under his arm. Then, he went out back, took two chairs and an end table off the patio, and brought them around, putting them in the truck. By the time he drove back down and put the furniture in place, Claire was cleaned up and stepping back outside. When she saw what he had done, she made an about-face back into the kitchen to bring out two wine glasses, an opener, and some candles. She also brought a board piled with cheeses and crackers, grapes, and pears. Thinking, *I'll even cook something next time.*

Chapter Sixteen

*D*uring the early part of June, they rode in silence, only talking when it was safe. The bugs were so thick this spring that opening their mouths was dangerous. These bugs couldn't be seen from a distance, but they were everywhere in huge swarms, just waiting for unassuming cyclists to open their mouths.

Riding along, they passed and saw in distant fields big wagons stacked with boxes. Ben explained these were boxes of bees; these were their hives. The closer they got a subtle, almost eerie, humming droned on, surrounding them and vibrating through the terrain. Claire didn't recognize the sound or sensation at first. The closer to the wagons they rode, the louder the hum became -- as they watched the swarming bees taking flight and returning to their hives. Farmers knew to let nature have her way. Certain vegetable plants needed to be pollinated to flower. The local beekeeper brought his hives out to the fields on a pay-to-pollinate basis. The bees flew in a mile radius from the hives, spending their days joyfully and busily at work, and the farmer watched his plants in the fields soon flourish and become heavy with vegetables.

Ben was the perfect navigator. How could he possibly know where every country road led? For the most part, though, he did. Still, never leaving the farm without a GPS seemed like a good idea to her. They rode deep through farmland, keeping away from packing houses, state roads, and busy township thoroughfares. Farm country traffic was heavy this time of year and would remain that way through October. But directly across Hwy 72 traffic seemed to stop and the land stretched out as if the universe had spread a glorious black and malachite patchwork quilt on the earth. There was one elevation which gave them a panoramic view. The farms that extended before them were bursting with activity. Since the middle of April planting had gone on ten and twelve hours a day, seven days a week, and continued until farmers were satisfied that their last fields had been seeded. Now, everywhere Claire looked was completely transformed. The fields which had spread out, acre upon acre, with perfect rows of rich black soil and young pale green shoots, had now delivered maturing vegetation. This place too was becoming transformative for her. *Nothing has changed outside, still squeamish as ever,* she smiled. *But, nothing appears the way I expected.* She took a deep breath, looking across the expanse as anonymous farmers were hard at work. She thought, *To be a good farmer a man had to be balanced -- openly giving his masculine and feminine traits full expression. With proper nurturing and care, man and nature linked in harmony. Man with a handful of seeds could lure her. She, nature -- the embodiment of life -- let him know they were interconnected and interdependent while abundantly displaying her masculine will and power, with feminine beauty and grace.*

Man had his masculine and feminine traits. Women were no different. Man had to be courageous, discerning, disciplined, focused, and persevering. And the strongest positive masculine trait of all was that he had to have faith -- in the land, in his equipment, and in himself. It was a powerful set of characteristics for any man or woman to possess. But that was only half the man.

His feminine side needed to express fully to get the job done. He had to love the land and love his family. He had to be flexible and accepting of the weather and challenges. He had to wait and be receptive, open to receive, as his crop germinated and grew to maturity. And his greatest feminine trait of all was to be at peace with himself and the world around him. This conveyed a picture Claire had never thought about before. She had never seen herself as connected to everything and everyone that lived, grew, or blossomed around her. Riding on, she smiled as this positive Yin Yang descriptive filled her heart. Her outlook on life amused even her at times.

It appeared farmers all know one another, and knew their fathers and their grandfathers before them. As they rode past farms Ben called off names and told anecdotal stories. Claire thought people in these small towns lived entirely too much in the past. Then again, she would tell herself, you had to keep history alive. These small towns along their rides were little time capsules, not having necessarily worn the years well. She considered most of them just needed a good can of white paint to liven them up! Much of it had an inbred quality, remaining separate from the vast world around them. Most who lived here had no desire to see or experience what was outside of their world. They celebrated together, wept together, gossiped together, and were always there to lend a hand.

Through Ben, Claire was meeting people who were originally from the town, had grown up on these farms, left, then returned. These expats left to follow their career paths, only to return years later. Certainly Ben was one of these. And she remembered the story he told about the Klaussen's. He also introduced Claire to a former classmate. He had run into Elizabeth a couple of years earlier, when she first returned to Salinger. They tried to date at the time, but quickly realized they were better at being friends. Elizabeth Stark graduated from Georgetown University, wanting to never look back at her humble Midwestern roots. She went on to a twenty-five year career as a Washington D.C. lobbyist. Having burned out on her career, she retired early and returned to build her dream farmhouse, one she had planned and envisioned all of her life. Liz inherited the land that her parents and grandparents had farmed. She had such sweet memories, or so they seemed in comparison to Washington, of a carefree childhood. She simply wanted to recover those feelings and hold on a little longer. She left the northeast corridor, returning to the Midwest only after the bumps and bruises became too many and the disappointments too profound. After two failed marriages and never taking the time to have children, she decided to move closer to family, close to her brother, sister-in-law, and her two nieces.

She looked forward to a new, simpler way of life. Void of the drudgery of snarled traffic jams, inflated egos, and overworked long days that spilled into the nights. Liz's home, too, looked like a time capsule. But that was the intention, and it was beautiful. Claire wondered, *What would she do after the house was finished? Why think that far ahead.* She enjoyed sitting in the parlor with Liz, as that was the first phase of the renovation. The house was being restored and expanded to an antebellum homestead. Her tastes were far more refined than her parents simple tastes had ever been. She wiped the slate clean and here was license to expand the farmhouse into her childhood dreams of a grand plantation home. Claire loved her restored innocence and spirit. In some ways, she reminded Claire of herself, maybe due to the hurts or the optimism she portrayed. The two were becoming fast friends.

Out to dinner one night, Ben saw an old friend sitting at one of the tables nearby and introduced Claire to him. John Holtz was a retired English professor who had also returned to Salinger. John's was much the same history as Liz's, except after college he moved to Wisconsin, where he remained on the faculty at the University of Wisconsin for twenty-seven years. Having just returned that summer, he told them he was still settling in. John had inherited the family farm, split it with his two sisters, and had come back to live and write his life's ambition, novel. Claire asked John if he was married and if he had children. She hadn't known Liz long but was already matchmaking. Ben was oblivious to what had just occurred. She made a note to self, *Introduce John to Liz. I wonder if they know one another.* She knew he had John's number and she had Liz's.

The restaurant had a terrace that extended over Lake Erie. After dinner they finished their wine outside. Tonight there was a band playing. Claire and Ben danced under the stars on the cool summer night. Flirting, moving, and being close every opportunity they found, they danced as if no one else was there. They stayed till the last song and walked back to the car holding hands. They were becoming good friends, but tonight was different. This was the first time he had shown any emotional interest. She could feel the gentle breeze brush her cheek and move through her hair. She looked up at him and he looked into her eyes. They both wanted this kiss. They had taken so long, as if afraid of knowing what would happen next. The chemistry had been there from the first day. His hand touched her cheek and he drew her to him. She got on her toes to meet his lips, wanting all of his mouth. He became lost in her soft, responsive lips. He thought of her often, but the messages she sent were often unclear. Tonight there was no mistaking her desires, and he took her in his arms. Embracing, her frame felt small, so feminine, yet her body was firm and athletic. She was not stepping away and neither was he. They each liked the way the other kissed. Driving back they talked about dinner and the dancing. Laughing, they remembered the waiter with the flourish who served them, and talked about where they would ride tomorrow. In silence, she thought, *maybe tonight wasn't such a good idea.* But she could not stop herself.

Chapter Seventeen

Cooking for one was proving quite impossible, and often she found herself eating leftovers with salads day after day. At home in Palm Beach her lifestyle was very different; between her work schedule, community service and events, and art exhibits, her days and evenings were always planned full and in advance, so she usually found herself eating out with friends. Knowing many of the restaurant owners by name she liked the attention and service they showed her. Farm life was very different than city life. Here, they had their best local restaurant, which happened to be The Country Inn Restaurant, several diners, and in nearby towns located right off the interstate there were the usual chain restaurants. The greater area was charming and there were some very good regional restaurants, but nothing close by or easy for takeout. That wasn't true any longer, she now knew of the Chinese restaurant. Unfortunately, sometimes when they ate out Ben had a far less discriminating palette than hers, so she was even eating fast food from time to time. She felt better and had more energy when she ate well -- ate the very foods surrounding her in the fields! She had been driving out of town to buy a good selection of fruits and vegetables, but now, out there all around were fresh vegetables of every variety, hers for the picking.

Later that next day, Charity was coming to lunch. Claire ate lunch alone most all the time, except Tuesdays when now Charity came over. Quitting at noon on those days gave Claire something to look forward to. Some weeks were harder than others. She didn't mind being alone. Traveling in her business put her alone often, but there was something very isolated about living here that she had not experienced before.

Having met Charity out a couple of times, Claire decided to invite her to the gatehouse. Having lunch out with her was like eating with the high school football team -- the greasier and fattier the better; so, for the sake of Claire's own health she told her guest it was no trouble for her; she enjoyed making lunch. At first Charity was a little intimidated, but looked forward to going to Claire's. Soon that led to surprise, even disappointment. She had hoped to finally see where Ben lived, assuming all along that Claire was Ben's girlfriend. It was a natural misunderstanding, she dismissed, since Claire was seen driving in and out of his driveway every day. The disappointment came when she found out that Claire was only a tenant at the farm. Charity had spread much of the gossip before Norma and Mat informed her why Claire was there. Like everything in her life these days, she felt like an out of control heel for doing that damage to Claire.

She now knew Claire was there to help them transition into a new child care facility and improve the level of education in the town. The residents were just hearing about the closing of the existing program, and there was a great deal of concern, even resentment. Sitting down Charity immediately became irate, as if she had to make a stand for the residents. Claire did not want to hear her verbose antics, assuring her the school board would be making their announcement soon.

Claire took this opportunity to ask Charity if she knew why people were not very friendly toward her. Charity looked her straight in the eyes," People aren't fond of Ben Donohue.

They don't know him anymore. Then he comes back giving charity to some families but he could do more, he could hire more of the men, or he could help this town more." said Charity emphatically.

Claire asked, "Does your farm hire more of the men from town? Or is that a local problem for all the bigger farms in the area?" Claire asked

"Mat hires about 50/50. It's a tough problem." Charity said

"Alright, but everything you've told me is about Ben. I asked about me." Claire brought their conversation back around.

"Well, I've heard people think you're his girlfriend. I didn't know there was another house on this property." Charity huffed, only afterwards realizing this came out wrong.

It made sense to Claire that her being seen coming and going from this driveway had to be driving the local residents crazy with curiosity.

Claire and Charity settled into their new routine on Tuesdays. At first, having Claire make lunch annoyed Charity. First of all she wanted to be seen with her, but also there were many things about Claire that annoyed her. She was too perfect, pretty, smart, and had a great job; yet she was kind and accepting. Charity had never experienced this before. The lunches tasted alright, although, not enough food and bland for sure. Last week it was a small omelet with a salad on the side. Tiny! Not like a Bob Evans omelet smothered in cheese and ham. Why did Claire have to be so different? Today lunch was tomato slices with white cheese in between the slices and fresh basil leaves layered between the cheese and tomato. Charity had never eaten raw basil, and thought she would gag. All the basil grown on the farms was sold to food companies where it was dried and packaged. Then, Claire poured a little olive oil over it and added salt and pepper. She called it an Italian name, a Calabrese Salad. Most everything had a name with Claire. All she put on salads was salt and pepper, some fresh herbs she grew in pots on the deck, and some olive oil with squeezed lemons as the salad dressing. At first this dressing had no flavor -- *no taste at all*, thought Charity. It was too simple, not creamy enough! If they were having a salad, she dreamed of her refrigerator at home with at least eight or ten varieties of salad dressings in the door. If she had to have a salad she would rather be having thousand islands or blue cheese dressing on it.

At first, Charity left hungry every week. She went home telling herself she was starving and couldn't wait to get home to make herself a sandwich; or she'd open a bag of chips, eating the whole thing. It seemed funny at first; she felt like an unruly child who was getting away with something.

But she was glad Norma had brought Claire to Salinger. Mat knew, but Charity hadn't told Norma yet that she was friends with Claire. She kept it as something special to which she could look forward. Not sure why, other than it was something different to do and made her feel important. And she didn't want Norma to start coming along. This was her special time, and nothing had felt special for a long time. At lunch, they would talk about the Center. Claire was open about all the steps and work that went into Salinger's new Children's Center. They talked about their children, the area, and places in Florida where Charity had vacationed. Claire wanted recipes, wanting to know what they cooked here. Charity wasn't impressed with Claire's cooking so didn't ask for hers.

Then all of that next week Charity was terribly depressed. She hated her body! She blew up at her daughter for a very small thing and regretted it for days. She felt she was out of control. Lunch was on Tuesdays at Claire's, and for some reason Charity could hardly wait to get there this week. She was fighting back the tears all morning long. As soon as she walked through the door she hugged Claire. Barely even knowing her she nonetheless felt Claire was her last hope. Almost pleading she said, "Please help me, help me lose weight, help me be happy again! Tell me if you can help, please." Claire was concerned about Charity, and saw she finally trusted her enough to feel safe, and speak her true feelings. Lunch was already sitting on the table. Claire had made a curried chicken salad on a mountain of soft bib lettuce. Claire said, "Life is a time to love more, and be filled with happiness, joy, pleasures, and desires."

That was it? What kind of advice is that? Bursting with frustration, Charity thought, *That's ridiculous! How am I supposed to lose 40 pounds on that advice?*

Claire smiled, "We're all responsible for our own happiness. When you feel how truly happy you are inside, things will start to change. Why don't you get started!"

Claire continued, "Start by listening to the way you speak to yourself. Listen first thing in the morning when you wake up. Catch yourself every time you aren't nice to yourself. Start listening and start changing the way you talk to you. Would you talk to a friend that way? Or would you let another person speak to you that way? You would probably walk away and not be their friend. No more being mean to you! No more angry chatter at anyone else either, but most of all, you. This week listen to what your mind is telling you, what the voice inside your head is saying. Be aware of what you are saying throughout the day. From time to time, stop and listen. Then several times a day, anytime you think of it, smile and tell yourself – 'I'm so happy!' Even if you don't mean it, even if you think you sound ridiculous, smile and say, 'I'm so happy!' Because eventually, it'll be true, and you won't be able to say the sentence without feeling good."

"That's it?" cried Charity.

"For now." Claire could see Charity was on the verge of tears.

How could this be all she had to say? That's the most ridiculous thing I've ever heard! Thought Charity, nonetheless, she told her all about how she felt about her weight. She couldn't tell her how sad she was about her marriage.

As she was leaving Charity could barely muster a smile and knew she had to get away from there. Furious, she talked to herself all the way home, *Claire was no help, not with advice like that! She's crazy.* She wasn't sure she would even go back.

So annoyed she committed to prove Claire completely wrong, Charity had her ears glued to her mind that night. This wasn't a big deal, and she thought she could easily control her mind. After all, she thought, she controlled everything else in her life. While getting ready for bed that night, she heard her mind say "you cow," and she noticed several other awful things she said to herself. It shocked her so much she was almost afraid to lie down. It was a terrible night. She kept fighting in her mind with herself, with Mat, with her daughters. In a dream, she stood up in a town meeting and screamed at the council members. She was out of control! She barely slept that night.

The next morning she jumped out of bed, though completely exhausted. Ignoring Claire's advice all of that day and the next, things got back to normal. Thank goodness, because that had been uncomfortable!

The weekend went by, and every now and then, she would listen in and heard how she berated herself. She thought about how stupid she sounded or that she was fat or ugly. What she heard was so upsetting. Once again, she was afraid to go to bed. The whole week had been a long, emotional roller coaster ride. Every now and then, she remembered and would snidely say "Oh, I'm so happy." Not believing a word, she noticed she had eaten all the cookies in the pantry that week.

RECIPES

Curried Chicken Salad:

1 cooked skinless, boneless chicken breast	2 celery stalks, washed and chopped
A handful of grapes, cut up	1+ tablespoon of mayonnaise
¼ teaspoon cumin	1 teaspoon curry powder
Salt and pepper to taste	

Cut up the cooked chicken, celery and grapes. In a separate bowl combine the mayonnaise, cumin, curry powder, salt and pepper. Mix together. Serves 2.

Chapter Eighteen

*B*en would plan the direction of their rides according to wind speed. By the afternoon, winds would whip up and they could expect 15-20 mile per hour wind gusts. Cycling into that kind of wind was hard work, and the combination of uphill climbing with the wind in their faces was doubly hard. As the weeks progressed, they both got stronger and found the rides were becoming longer and easier. Cycling was definitely breaking the ice. It was melting the guarded exterior of the strong and private man. Simply going with the flow and doing what she loved drew him closer every day. They were having so much fun together. Most days when Ben returned from the farm they had already talked, and Claire would ride up the driveway to meet him. Each time she got off her bike, his eyes went straight to her body. He tried to be discrete but felt drawn to her sensuality, and liked her in riding shorts. All Claire thought of when she got on her bike was *thank goodness for padded shorts and gloves*. She did not want calluses on her hands or anywhere else on her soft skin.

They usually took his hybrid bicycles on these rides across the miles of farmland. The hybrids were more forgiving. Many of the roads were uneven, and there were potholes here and there. Frequently, there was also the danger of a driver who would get too close while driving too fast and practically run them off the road. All they could do was quickly duck onto the gravel shoulder. That was always a scary moment, and it didn't take very long to figure out it usually occurred on Friday evenings. The beauty of riding these back roads was they barely passed any cars. Occasionally a semi was stopped on the shoulder of the road in front of a house. Some days they would count fewer than ten cars during a fifteen or twenty mile ride. Other times, amazingly, they would be passed by even fewer vehicles. But for some reason on Fridays, after 5 p.m., every fast-moving pickup truck in the county came barreling down the road. Soon they figured this pattern out and attributed it to this being payday, so Fridays became a good day to take off from riding. Claire took one other day off as well.

As much as they rode the hybrids, she was sure Ben would prefer to be riding his road bike, a racing bike, exclusively if she wasn't there. Most people she knew who cycled loved their road bikes. The exhilaration and fast speeds were the rush most people looked forward to. She liked her road bike, too; it was a completely different ride. Having both options let them mix up the rides, making them both happy. With the road bike, it took more concentration on the art of cycling, the road, and on the equipment itself.

On a road bike, you focused on aerodynamics; locking into the pedals, you had to trust your equipment. Next, you tucked your body into the bike, down low and centered forward over your handlebars and skinny wheels. Cycling reminded her of skiing; lean your body forward and fly down the mountain. That was what she loved about skiing. She loved the fearless rush, leaning downhill even when you really wanted to sit back on your skis. There was another similarity between cycling and skiing. All of your attention was focused on the road in front of you, with little margin for error --

quick jolts, little rocks, an unsteady skid on gravel, or maybe a sudden pothole -- any one of these could blow a tire. And just like quick release bindings on your skis, the quick release on your pedals was the difference between injury, or just another good cycling story if something or someone pulled out in front of you. That's how you prepared psychologically every time you got on the road bike -- you were in your Tour de France mode hoping to average eighteen-plus miles per hour on extended rides.

Claire absolutely enjoyed the racing bike kind of cycling, but her favorite was the hybrid ride. There was more forgiveness. The tires were fatter, and the handle bars let you ride sitting straight up. This ride was about the adventure as the bike could take the road stress. Taking this ride was much more of a workout. More calories and energy were expended because of the fatter wheels and the bulkier bicycle frame. It was also a slower ride. The hills were harder to climb, and going downhill you didn't get up to the same speeds. She never got over twenty-one miles per hour going downhill, but that was fast enough for her. A good ride was going twelve to fifteen miles per hour through the country while watching everything around them -- being the journey.

Quietly cycling through the landscape the summer brought harvests wherever they rode. Within weeks she watched the wheat go from short green grass, to emerald green stalks, to shiny gold shafts in the sunlight. They stayed as such for several weeks, and then suddenly transformed to an ancient bronze patina. Soon after, loud combines thundered through; harvested bales were packed tightly then hauled away, and the fields lay silently empty again. Nature could not rest yet; this time of year she had to immediately prepare for her encore performance. The fields were immediately replanted in alternate rows from where the wheat had stood, this time with soybeans. Cut down wheat stalks still stood a few inches tall while they died. The alternate rows erupted in bright emerald greens. Soon, the soybean plants grew above the short wheat stalks and a dense green, leafy blanket covered the earth. The landscape around the cyclists had changed again, rapidly evolving and maturing.

Claire discovered she loved being outdoors. She loved looking up at the moon and stars, feeling the sun upon her, and looking out across the fields. It was like the feelings she had while at the beach. She felt the same level of peace as she looked out over her world either here in Ohio or Florida. That was strange; she had not thought in those terms before.

Riding through the miles of still countryside, the silence was only broken by the wind rustling through the fields, an eruption of crickets chirping, or by dogs barking. Farmers on tractors worked the land from early morning till late at night. Blaring activity then led to an extended hush of silence as the land was left to its own devices, while it was carefully and attentively being monitored and maintained until it was ready to harvest. Ben would tell her field facts as they rode through the country. He wanted her to know and understand his world and be a part of it, if that was possible.

To Claire, this practical information described Nature's way of giving birth to her abundance. *The farmer became a surrogate parent to all the varied possibilities in demonstrating her bounty. His DNA was evidenced in the seeds he chose to plant, in his fields, and in how he nurtured these seeds with water, soil, nutrients, sunlight, and faith in the process. In essence he was raising his family again. Every seed he planted was highly important to him; yet he knew some seeds would grow and some wouldn't. In a corn field, around 25,000 seeds went into an acre of land. He made a commitment to nurture each stalk as it grew, since his life and livelihood depended on these seedlings surviving.* This gave Claire pause as she thought, *Aren't we fertile ground? How many ideas and desires do we plant? 25,000 seeds? And don't some grow and some just don't.*

Where the bees had been busy a few short weeks before, there were now plants abundantly endowed with blossoms and vegetables; beautiful squashes, zucchinis, peppers, and cucumbers. When they took a break to have a drink and stretch their legs, Claire bent down to look at the flowers and thought the vegetables seemed almost out of place. She kept a small nylon backpack in her saddle bag and those nights when they passed a zucchini field she took a few back home. That evening she boiled the just-picked zucchini for five minutes, simply long enough to soften them. She cut them long ways in half and scooped out the centers. Next, piling the centers high with a mixture of chopped tomatoes, green onions, parsley, cilantro, peppers, and cheddar cheese, she then sprinkled them with salt and pepper, fresh thyme and oregano from her garden. She placed them under the broiler for ten minutes, until the cheese melted. Dinner was ready.

Her ease in the kitchen came back quickly, and she was having fun. Like this one, all her old favorite recipes were coming back to her and she was back to cooking with a little of this and a sprinkle of that. On late nights after a good ride this was how they ate. And there was always crusty whole grain bread with olive oil, and a glass of one of their favorite wines. It was good to have a partner with whom to share this pleasure. Ben was no longer content to treat this only as a growing friendship. They appeared to come from different worlds, causing him to hesitate. He decided he did not want to waste time and risk losing her by waiting -- waiting to see if this winter they would possibly plan to visit one another again. That was their original aim, feeling that it would be appropriate to wait until after the project was over, and then consider if they wanted to see more of each other. *Why was that so important?* He thought.

They had both been careful not to blur the lines between their personal and professional relationship. She was here as a paid consultant, and he was potentially her biggest donor. Claire had to be careful not to appear to be behaving inappropriately, and Ben had to respect professional boundaries. This was a risk he decided he needed to take. Weeks before, completely out of character, he had a crazy, momentary notion: *I'm going to marry her.*

There was more for Ben, though. He was pragmatic with everything in his life. Besides considering their professional association, he wanted to be comfortable before speaking out; he wanted to feel sure that he could bridge the divide between their worlds. Ben often thought about how this could work. He had traveled the world through his business yet was always most comfortable in his own environment and his own industry. He knew the people of Palm Beach to be more diverse, more social, and a lot showier. He wanted her to be happy, yet he questioned: could he make her happy and still remain true to himself?

This woman disarmed him, he thought. She moved through her work and her life as though she was simply open to enjoying the pleasures and resolving the conflicts as they came along. She could be walking through a field assessing in her own way how the crop looked -- making him laugh with her assessments; then just as quickly challenging him to observe and think more deeply while he listened to her spiritual insightfulness. Moments later, she could be on the phone as if a thousand miles away or back in Palm Beach. She was in one moment strong, resourceful, and laser direct. Then, just as quickly becoming his muse, an angel dropped from heaven.

After a long ride and dinner, they always parted ways. Tonight Claire stayed. Ben asked, "What do you want, Claire?"

She replied, "I want to finish the project. I think it's going to be impactful not only for Salinger but for the whole region."

"That's not what I mean. Why do you keep running away?" he pressed.

"I'm not running away!" she snapped back.

"You are so good to others. I see the effect you have on those around you. Why won't you stop and be good to yourself, too?" He continued, "How many relationships have you turned away? Don't do that here, not without at least giving this one a chance." He blurted out, "Claire, I'm falling in love with you! And it kills me you might not give us a fair chance."

Claire's eyes welled up. Wasn't that what she had been longing to hear? With a little smile she thought, *Listen girl, careful what you wish for, it can be a thought away.*

She didn't hesitate this time, and kissed him, and could feel her heart expand and her chest flush. Her kiss always excited him, and both sank into the very special way they felt when they kissed. Something had shifted when Ben spoke out. This kiss felt different, captivating, and both of them felt a new beginning ahead. They had wanted each other for a very long time.

This night she did not leave to go home. And yes, disarming him again, she had asked for a blood test recently, and he quickly obliged. He knew he had no diseases, but was charmed by her self-awareness and self-respect. He honored her request and gave her the paper with the results; then simply waited for her to be ready. This night he smiled and said he had a special surprise for her. He disappeared for a few minutes, and then guided her to the bathroom, where, with candles lit, he had drawn a hot bath for her and turned the jets on which frothed the sumptuous, aromatic bath salts he'd bought her. Ben went to the other bathroom. Claire sank into the salts and bubbles, allowing the hot water to massage her back and shoulders, her hips and thighs. It washed over her fatigued muscles, relaxing her whole body. She took a hot washcloth and covered her face and rested her eyes breathing in the calming lavender salts. They had ridden twenty-two miles this night. Getting out of the tub, she toweled off. The mineral salts had left her skin feeling soft and smelling good.

Stepping into the bedroom, Ben watched her graceful body as she came around the bed and sat next to him as if she simply wanted to look at him. On this clear summer night, as the moonlight peered through the open windows, she could smell the clean air and could feel the gentle breeze tingle on her skin. The moon softly lit the room, and they could see each other clearly, could see into each other's eyes. He was admiring her body and traced his hand up her leg, over her hip, and found her hand, drawing her close. As they sank into each other's arms and hearts, their bodies felt the pleasure of their closeness, and the genuine tenderness of their caress let the other know this was love. The trees outside the window swayed to the wind, and the moonlight played to Claire and Ben's passionate motion.

Chapter Nineteen

"*I*'ve hardly slept all week!" Charity groaned. Tuesday had finally come again. Claire listened sympathetically as Charity described her awful week.

"This week keep listening to yourself. Notice what you're thinking. Make a point that if you are resentful, angry, or critical of yourself or someone else, stop right there. Tell yourself, 'Cancel that!' so you get yourself back in the present moment. Start living in the present. Stay present to your thoughts and emotions. And just be nice to yourself. Speak kind words. Change the way you talk to yourself. Stay out of the past – that's over -- and the future hasn't happened yet. Stay right where you are, present to yourself."

Charity chided, "What about the weight? I know that's my whole problem. If I could just get rid of this body, everything would be fine!"

Claire said, "Alright, catch yourself; every time you say something about your body, or you put yourself down, follow it up with, 'Not true, I love and appreciate myself.' Even if you don't believe it yet, even if you think you sound crazy, stop and say, 'I love and appreciate myself.'"

Leaving Charity alone for a couple of minutes, Claire walked out to the kitchen and returned with lunch, commenting, "Tarragon chicken salad is one of my favorites." This time the chicken salad was on a mountain of endive and baby green onions, with fresh dill tarragon vinaigrette.

Charity looked down at her plate, on the pretty table setting and cloth napkins and said, "You dropped grapes in the salad, you know."

"I don't know what you mean? You mean the grapes in this salad? Is there a whole grape in yours? I must have missed it. They're there on purpose. I put them in there. You are kidding, right?"

"I'm just sayin' I've never had this before!" Frustrated and on the verge of tears, she didn't recognize herself and the feelings she was having. When she was with Claire nothing ever tasted or seemed the way she had experienced anything in her life. Being with Claire was, she imagined, like being in a foreign country. Everything about her was completely different than Charity had ever known before in a person. And right now she felt like walking out.

She couldn't tell anyone she was listening to what this woman, this stranger, had to say. Nor would she tell anyone what they talked about. It was all too woo-woo! Claire was probably one of those people who read her horoscope every day, Charity thought. She was sure she would have never listened to anyone like this before in her life. But she was desperate. Something about Claire made her feel as if she could trust her and that she cared. Charity hadn't felt this safe with anyone in a long time. She could never have imagined how amazing it would feel to know someone cared about how she felt about herself.

True, she felt a little guilty about this, but Claire set her straight on that one. "No guilt – it's natural and so important to be your own best friend, first and foremost. You grew up taking care of everyone around you and overlooking the most important relationship of all -- the one with yourself." Claire would say.

Maybe this was just the permission Charity needed to allow her to take care of Charity, too. What Claire was saying was starting to make sense one time, and sounded preposterous the next. Charity began telling herself she deserved to be happy and could not sit waiting for others to make her happy, because so far that wasn't working. That's when she lost control and began sobbing as she thought of all the times Mat wanted to make her happy, but she did not react. She was lost, and frightfully, was enjoying her own suffering.

This began a deluge of tears and emotions. One week after the other Charity felt engulfed with sadness. She even began hating Claire for what was happening to her and she found excuses to stay away from her. "Ok, but call me if you need to talk." Claire had said. Just in case Claire was right, Charity kept insuring her progress by saying, "Cancel that crazy thinking and Oh, I love and appreciate myself."

She tried ignoring the feelings, cramming them back down every time something surfaced, but that hurt more now than ever. Finally when she thought she would burst the way the reservoir had years before flooding Pate's farm, she could not hold the dam back any longer. It began to overflow. Claire had said, "If you allow your emotions to come up, and you recognize the feelings you are having about a situation or a person; sit there and look at what you are feeling. As you shine a light on the situation or relationship; without judging it or yourself -- that light is love."

RECIPES

Tarragon Chicken Salad:

1 cooked, skinless, boneless chicken breast	2 celery stalks, washed and chopped
Handful of red seedless grapes, cut up	1-2 tablespoons mayonnaise
¾ teaspoon dried tarragon	4 tablespoon olive oil
Scant ½ teaspoon Dijon mustard	Juice of ½ lemon
A handful of fresh dill, chopped	Salt and pepper
Endive lettuce	2 scallions, chopped

Chop and combine chicken breast, celery, and grapes. Blend in the mayonnaise, ½ teaspoon tarragon, salt and pepper. Mix the chicken salad and refrigerate for at least 30 minutes. Wash and place the endive lettuce in a bowl. Add the scallions. In a separate small bowl make the dressing by first wisking together the olive oil and mustard. Add lemon juice, ¼ teaspoon tarragon, dill, salt and pepper. Blend well. Using the dressing toss the salad. Plate the greens and add a scoop of chicken salad on top. Serves 2.

Chapter Twenty

*B*y the latter part of June, Ben and Claire were riding a hundred miles per week. Watching the fields, they witnessed as the thousands of acres of maturing crops along the miles and miles of country roads gave way to harvests all summer long. They usually rode at least ten miles in one direction. Then they would stop to stretch, and sit on a bridge or a rock as they drank and talked. Layers of their lives were peeling away, making each completely comfortable with the other.

Some days he was warm and affectionate, but others he pulled back. She didn't know if she had said something or if he was having a bad day. For days now, she noticed him withdraw, and they each went to their own homes after their rides. She felt sad. "Ben, why are you so distant?"

His response came quickly, "You're leaving soon. Come on, let's ride. Let me show you something."

Back on their bikes, they went down Bauer Road. There the farm stretched out in front of them. Riding up, the field appeared as if it held rows and rows of pampered, gentle green velvet. She didn't recognize what this was at first; these were lush mounds of frilly leaf lettuces side by side in red and green rows, mounded up nearly two feet tall. Next to them grew bib lettuce. Its delicate leaves were nearly translucent and sensually folded open, looking buttery soft. Another field was brimming with romaine and escarole. Romaine appears as blooms, fanning out like large rose petals, open and fleshy to the sunlight. Claire thought. *How sensual and sultry nature is when she shows off her best.*

Tomorrow would be Tuesday, and she and Charity were having spinach, mushroom, and beet salad with more of the fresh dill-tarragon vinaigrette. Margarita pizza made on whole wheat pita bread would finish off lunch.

They stopped and filled her backpack with fresh vegetables. Claire was getting good at making a clean cut when she harvested vegetables from the ground. The secret was to keep your wide face knife very sharp and come across squarely in one stroke. It was like a machete chop. She loved the sound of the fresh, bursting snap. The earth opened up and birthed something majestic wherever she looked. She was now a fixture in the fields every other day, bringing home fresh herbs and vegetables. The best time to cut fresh vegetables was after 7 p.m., after the heat of the day subsided. The lighting in the fields at that time of day was dramatic and had a dance all its own. It reflected the subtle folds of the leaves and the different shades of green from pastels to deep forest hues. Every day the fields looked different. The place where she cut endive yesterday held no assurance that there would be any sign of endive there tomorrow. She would either have to go looking for another field or have a different lettuce. She was having so much fun!

There were days when she would look out in a field and see thirty acres of dense spinach rows. Then it would all be gone the next day. It was the same with the little green onions. Right next to the scallions, there were twenty acres of cilantro and massive fields of parsley stretched all around.

The parsley and cilantro they chopped re-grew like grass, springing back within days and growing back again and again all summer long. There were root vegetables, including the fifty-plus acres of beets, both red and yellow. She pulled them out of the ground. Below the broad leaves and red stalks were earth covered sweet luscious beets. There was also thirty acres planted in canning dill just for the pickle industry, next to that field was the delicate fluttering dill. The smell of dill was intoxicating and gave every dish a rich aroma. She could not help herself and put it in everything. Tonight they were having beans and greens in a light broth with veal meatballs. They dipped crusty rye bread in the broth, and had a good bottle of chilled Cake Bread Chardonnay.

Over dinner Ben called himself a gambler, saying all farmers were gamblers, but they had learned to play the odds -- knowing how to handle nature. She was good and gave to him with total abandon -- shining her sun, delivering her rain, and bringing balance between the insect world, the earth, and his needs. He would hit big or he could lose big. It didn't happen often, but every farmer had his story of the one or more bad years that nearly put him out of business. From one year to the next, the variables could change. It could be the weather, the soil, or the plants could be close to harvest when a disease manifested and spread. The markets could change, and earlier harvests in other parts of the country could impact his market value with their abundance or scarcity. A farmer could buy the newest invention in seed technology guaranteed to manage nature -- man exerting power over the elements. He could entice nature to yield more, to grow a heartier plant, but if she wasn't playing that season, a frost, a drought, or maybe too much rain could wipe him out.

They were having dinner on the patio. Staring out on the fields she watched a deer family feasting on baby onions at dusk, she was sure she missed something he had said.

RECIPES

Spinach, mushroom, and beet salad with more fresh dill-tarragon vinaigrette:

4 beets, about a pound	1/3 cup olive oil
4 tablespoons balsamic vinegar	Salt and pepper
Baby spinach leaves	8-10 white cap mushrooms, sliced thin

Tarragon Vinaigrette:

4 tablespoons olive oil	Juice of ½ lemon
Scant ½ teaspoon Dijon mustard	½ teaspoon tarragon
Small bunch of dill, chopped	Salt and pepper

Wash and trim the tops of the beets. In a pot of water, boil the beets until tender, about 45 minutes. Test with a fork. When the beets are cool enough, peel off the outer skin and cut them up into small wedges. Wisk the oil and vinegar, salt and pepper together. Toss the beets in the oil and vinegar dressing. You can make these up to two days ahead.

Fill your salad bowl with baby spinach, or in combination with arugula. Add the sliced mushrooms, beets, and toss with tarragon vinaigrette dressing. Serves 4.

Margarita Pizza Made on Whole Wheat Pita Bread:

2 Pita bread rounds
1 large tomato, sliced thin
¾ cup of shredded
mozzarella cheese
Oregano, salt and pepper

1 teaspoon olive oil
Fresh basil leaves, shredded
¼ cup parmesan cheese

Pick soft pita bread. Place it on a broiler pan. Brush the oil on the pitas. Arrange half of the tomatoes on the pitas. Top with the shredded basil, salt and pepper. Add the shredded cheese over the tomatoes and add remaining tomatoes on top of the cheese. Sprinkle with parmesan cheese, oregano, salt and pepper. Place under the broiler for 5 minutes or until cheese is lightly brown and melted.

Beans and Greens with Meatballs:

1 16 oz. can Great Northern Beans

1 clove of garlic

Enough olive oil to coat the saucepan

1 scant teaspoon oregano

1/3 lb ground veal

3-4 cups of spinach

Grated parmesan cheese

½ onion, minced

1 stalk of dill, chopped (optional)

1½ - 2 cups chicken stock

Salt and pepper

Wash and drain the beans. Sauté the onions and garlic in olive oil. Add the beans, dill, and oregano. Cook and stir for 2 minutes to lightly brown the beans with the onions. Be careful not to mash too many of the beans. Add the chicken stock and let boil. Simmer on medium heat for 5 minutes. Take the veal and make quarter size meatballs and drop them in the broth. Continue cooking for 30 minutes more. Add salt and pepper to taste. If your stock is salted no need to season your meatballs or add additional seasoning. If more broth is desired add additional stock. 2 minutes before serving add handfuls of spinach. This depends on how much spinach you like. We like a lot. Stir in the spinach and let it just barely wilt. Serve immediately. Sprinkle with parmesan cheese. Serves 2.

Chapter Twenty-One

*I*t did not matter what other vegetables they were harvesting on the farm; the fresh onion smell rested in the air. It was not an obtrusive smell, instead you could smell the onions growing. Besides the smell, there were onion skins everywhere. Whenever she got into his pickup truck, she first had to dust the skins off the seat. They were everywhere it seemed.

Claire knew the obvious, because onions store well they were a year-round commodity. While his harvest yielded a five month supply stored, stocked, and ready for distribution, in the off season the packing house was always stocked with onions he brokered from other parts of the country. He shipped all over the Midwest and Northeast. Trucks came to the farm and picked up loads all day long. The last truck left the loading dock by 6 p.m. If a driver had to drive all night to deliver his load to Philadelphia or New York by four the next morning, he needed to be on the road right after picking up his shipment. He had to get to his destination even earlier than 4 a.m. to get a place in line.

Because of this tight timeline, seeing trucks leave the packing house then seeing them still around town later made

Ben very uneasy. Seeing a truck parked either by the side of the road or in a driveway was an anomaly. Yet he was aware of seeing this far too often. Already this summer he had had four truckloads of onions returned with loads not delivered to their destinations. It was not good for business, and this disturbed him because these events were out of his control.

After dinner they often sat outside looking up at the stars, with nothing hindering the view of millions of stars stretched across the sky. Ben had had another incident that morning and began explaining, "It's so easy. We make it so attainable to be enterprising in this country, and the interstate trucking system is the perfect vehicle. Hearing the horrors of the Mexican drug cartels and trafficking crimes, we think it can only be happening in the big cities. Those drugs have to get to the big cities first, and there is a lot of demand once they arrive. So a secure pipeline needed to be established. Much of the drug business is run by Mexicans here. The illegal workers, as well as green card workers, are incentivized to become a part of these illicit drug operations. It's easy money and becomes a built-in safety net, keeping the worker in this country. They make a far better living than picking fruits or vegetables, so they can send money back home to their families or live better here. It really is clever, and, of course, the farmers have no idea when this is going on."

He continued, "Big farms used to own their own trucks. They could afford to own them outright and keep hired drivers. Traffic and logistics used to be kept in-house. Over ten years ago, it became too expensive to own and operate a fleet of trucks. Farmers have for some time now depended on independent truckers or small trucking companies to transport for them. Once a truck leaves the packing house, a farmer can only assume his load is bound for its destination.

Regardless of where onions are stored or shipped from, it is these loads that are the easiest to hide drugs in. The smell alone masks any other smell that could be hidden on a truck. It is the perfect conveyance."

He was adamant that the farmers were not in on it in any way. But from time to time, as a load was returned, they were unfortunately caught in the middle. It was an annoyance and bad business having a truck that was bound for a commercial wholesale distribution point in Detroit, New Jersey, New York, or even bound for any large mass merchandising distribution center to be sent back. These were high volume clients who expected their orders to arrive on time. Instead, they would receive a phone call from Ben saying they would receive a discount for their trouble because the truck had broken down. In fact, it had been sent back to Salinger because the Interstate Highway Commission and DEA confiscated drugs bound for interstate trafficking. The truckers were not held responsible, either. They were as caught off guard as the farmer. A third party somehow planted the drugs on the truck and the trail was cold. There was no trail back to an origin or going to a destination.

Farmers were on the phones at all times finding empty trucks to transport their orders. Trucks lined up all day as the orders came in. It was the farmers who did business year round, with whom the independent truckers wanted to be associated. But somewhere between when the load was packed and when it arrived, drugs became an affiliate cargo. Wherever onions were bound, there were distribution channels. And how they got into the United States in the first place was easy. They came up on produce delivery trucks from Mexico, bound for distribution points throughout the country. Since they carried perishables, border patrol let them pass with far less scrutiny than other deliveries. In the spring, these trucks were bound for towns in Texas. Later in the fall it was Midwestern towns. It could be anywhere in the country, and towns like Salinger had a booming drug trade because distribution channels began and intersected right there. This was how drugs could get anywhere.

Claire thought how in agriculture timing was everything, so the drug traffickers had an ideal distribution system to exploit. Big produce distributors and grocery chains kept their pipelines full as they fed the whole of the American population. Drugs were delivered to the depot and unpacked on the other side by the cartel's inside people, their Primo, keeping distribution in place and supplied. Trucks were on the road twenty-four-seven, keeping the pipeline intact and rarely disturbed.

Chapter Twenty-Two

*J*ust back from Indianapolis again the night before, Claire was finishing up in the office. "Off-Campus for Kids" had officially opened in Indianapolis that week. She remained at the school during the first four days of the open house. While the owners and their staff were now open for business, their marketing efforts had been successful and student enrollment was already filled. Now they were taking applications in the event of cancellation. And they were already discussing another possible location with Claire.

It was Tuesday, and there was no time to make lunch today. She had a meeting with Norma right after seeing Charity. With so much on her mind this morning, and being off schedule for the last few days, Claire had a hard time settling into her meditation that morning. Some days it was hard to let go of all of the thoughts swirling around in her head; difficult to quiet her mind and become still. *Ok, so that's our topic today – finding peace.* She smiled. Claire knew that Charity was ready to trust her next steps. Shaking her head with a smile, she also knew Charity would probably resist the suggestion at first. Ironically, Claire was not sure if she was amused by or curious about Claire; or if, whether truly aware of it or not, she was following her inner compass to take further steps along on her own spiritual path because it called her. Witnessing the changes in her friend, Claire could only be there to love and support her. *We really are no different from one another, all people. We all come here to grow -- and that's what makes us all the same.*

She was seeing the growth which she had experienced now occurring for Charity. Claire, who was always the student in the past, had now become the teacher. Yet, at the same time as she was transitioning in her own life this summer, she felt like the student once more. Smiling, she reflected, *Just when I think I have a grasp on life and feel somewhat wise and in control again, bam! Something unexpected comes along and disrupts it all.* The clash between living in her existing world and stepping out of her comfort zone to explore something unfamiliar became a catalyst for change, again. She was feeling new and vulnerable and thought, *We think we understand -- then something comes and reveals what we didn't know we still needed to understand.*

Remembering well her own journey it took Claire time to transition into the person she was today. The better she felt meant the better her life became. Then she added meditation, and it put a space between actions and events. It shifted the movie of her life into slow motion and helped Claire unravel the circumstances. Then the picture began changing, becoming brighter and clearer.

Reflecting back on prior years she remembered it was like starting over. Beginning anew suddenly became exciting and inspiring. And she discovered she could start over anytime she felt like it. She began living in the present and listened in to what the voice in her head was saying. She was astonished at the bad advice it had given her. One day she burst out laughing, finally saying, *Cancel that crazy thinking!* She was making herself crazy with her belief she somehow had failed everyone. *Hello in there! James and I were both responsible for what happened, and we are now both free to live successful and happy lives. Our children are grown, our house sold, and we are both healthy.* What a day it was when she realized this, and she became instantly grateful for the way it made her feel. She forgave herself and James. It took a long time to let go. She held on to it until it just didn't feel good to hold on to anymore. She forgave herself for the way she had treated herself. Forgave herself for the way she felt about him, for the ways she acted in the end, and forgave him for all the terrible things he said to her. She let him go and felt peaceful inside.

It was as if one day she had unlocked a doorway to happiness and stepped through to the other side. It was a bright and sunny place, and there just happened to be a beach there. Thinking about the mental exercise she used to do with her children, she soon discovered she would pick herself to be her own best friend, knowing it was a good barometer. She liked the person she had gotten to know. She was happy whether she was alone or with others. She gave her heartfelt best to everyone and to whatever she did. And no longer did she feel lonely or afraid. There was nothing to be afraid of. She remembered this was a milestone and a life altering shift.

She knew it was one thing to come up with these ideals and sparks of enlightenment, but living them in the real world was a daily challenge. She had been good to herself after that. She forgave herself and anyone who she felt had ever made her feel less than perfect. She knew her well-being was much deeper than how she exercised and what she ate. *It's what we think, how we feed our minds and our hearts. It's feeling what feeling happy actually feels like.*

Parking the car, she ran into Maryann's Sandwich and Gifts. Charity was already in line, so they picked up sandwiches and walked a couple of blocks to the park. Claire asked Charity if she had ever meditated.

"You mean like in the movies or the show I watched when I was a kid called *Kung Fu*? Yes Grasshopper, no Grasshopper. I don't even know why they called him Grasshopper. Claire, you scare me sometimes. Don't be so weird! Here goes, ok, why should I?"

Claire described it as a calm feeling she could rest in. "It's a change agent." Claire knew she lost her there. Better to say, "With meditation, you could come to know yourself better. It can help you be more patient, and it helps calm down your busy mind. Another big benefit is at the cellular level -- its anti-aging." Claire assured her it was not a giant mystery or against her church upbringing, and she should just try it for three weeks. "Why three weeks?" asked Charity.

Claire replied, "They say that's how long it takes for a new habit to become ingrained. If you make yourself do it, it will become easier and easier to come back to."

Charity had never thought these ideas were anything to which to aspire, much less that she could achieve them or that they would be a way to feel settled or more patient. "Heck, I'm open minded!" They both burst out laughing. Claire described every day for twenty-one days she should give herself fifteen or twenty minutes to settle down and just relax. The best way to assure she would come back to it the following day was by committing to do the practice at the same time every day. They finished lunch then Claire said, "Let's get started."

The girls sat across from one another. "Take a few deep breaths." Claire showed her, and as she inhaled through her nose her stomach protruded out. On the exhale her stomach contracted inward. Charity said trying to breathe this way did not feel natural. Claire reminded her of her grandchildren's magnificent little bodies and how they breathed deeply, from their bellies. "Spending our adult lives holding in our stomachs, we forgot how to breathe deeply and end up taking shallow breaths up in our chest instead of engaging our full bodies. Practice -- focus and coordinate your stomach action with your breath. Soon it will feel natural again. Try it -- on the inhale push out your stomach. When you release that deep breath, pull your stomach in. Allow your stomach to contract." Charity promised herself she would practice this.

Claire began, "Lightly close your eyes or just let your eyes soften, and count your breaths. Inhale on the count of one, exhale on two. Concentrate on your breaths and count them from one to ten. If your mind wanders off, just begin again. One to ten, then begin again. Keep doing this, and simply start over every time your mind goes off and starts thinking about something else. That's it. Just do this for three weeks. This gives you something to do and a way to slow your busy mind. Later, after you've been counting for a while, you may want to do more. Think of the love you feel for your grandchildren, or how you feel holding puppies. Experience that feeling and try to hold on to it inside. Hold that feeling as long as you can. Keep bringing it back into your body. Feel it radiating in and out and through. Feel how joyful, peaceful, loving that is. Every time your mind takes you away just start over. Bring yourself back by counting. It's not a big deal. There's no wrong way to do it. You'll see what works for you. It isn't easy at first. Your mind will do all it can to distract you, but stay there and just start over. Let your body come to know the peace that lives inside you."

Feeling awkward, Charity said, "Ok, I'll seriously try it."

Chapter Twenty-Three

*C*laire liked what cycling was doing for her body. She always had a reasonably pretty figure from exercising regularly, but age fifty-one was giving her hips a certain mature womanly roundedness. Cycling was changing this shape. Her hips were becoming narrower and her stomach flatter. Her arms were stronger and there was more definition. Her back was muscular again, too. Her legs were stronger now. All over, her body was firming up it seemed, from the inside out. Their rides were getting longer and the days were hotter, yet the rides had gotten easier. She was feeling, *Oh so good!*

Getting an early start on Sunday morning, they planned to take a thirty mile ride. Church was the big open sky and tapestry of colors below. Cycling along these narrow roadways, they pedaled past pampered fields of lush green and flaxen gold, brilliant blue horizons, and towering cumulus clouds. Coming up on a little forest of trees, they rode through a passage of cooled balmy air. It flooded back memories of Europe. *This piece of the planet could just as easily be in parts of France, Italy, or Germany.* Pedaling, she reminisced about her trip through Tuscany. Admittedly, she had never seen very much of her own country, mostly choosing to travel abroad. Within the United States, she visited some major cities and landmark areas, went back to Mackinac Island several times, and flew by helicopter over the Grand Canyon. But to make a trip to rural Ohio was never a priority nor had it implied a certain romantic charm.

Today was their All-American ride; cycling along in early July, the corn fields were already shoulder high. The fields of corn stalks grew strong and had suddenly come alive. In her field facts she discovered the crop was becoming sexually active. The (male) tassels, which had grown tall out of the tops of the stalks only the week before, were freely and deliberately dropping their pollen with every puff of wind. Below, the ears were awake, open, and swaying, showing off their frilly silk expressions. The silk (female) had a soft pale, lacy quality at first, while the corn was young and glistening under the Sunday morning sky. The two got off their bikes, stopping to drink, and watched the dance the wind, pollen, tassels, and silk all did together. It was nature's dance of mind, heart, body, and spirit. To Claire, the silk of the plants looked like little sensual ballerinas kicking up their legs. And no, Ben had never thought of vegetables that way! Her observations and the correlations she described never ceased to amaze and amuse him.

He went over and pulled a baby ear off its stalk, unfurling the leaves gently to expose the baby kernels. Each kernel had a silk strand attached to it. It fed the kernel and resembled an umbilical cord. *Corn gave birth and nurtured its fruits to maturity like we do.* She thought.

They were on their way to Ward's Crossing for breakfast. The diner they liked to stop at was built in 1952 and much of it had not been renovated since. There were two window air conditioners, one at either end of the building. The countertop laminate surface had been replaced in 1984. The chairs and tables were replaced as they broke. The kitchen had received a new vent and griddle back in 2002. It was a landmark, but it was not at all fair to call it a greasy spoon. The waitress Jeannie owned the diner. The coffee was terrible. *Sorry Jeannie*, thought Claire, but she always rushed over with two mugs, quickly pouring a cup as soon as the sweaty duo with the helmet hair walked into the place. She had bought the diner eight years ago so she could afford to put her son and daughter through college. Breakfast was always good, and she served the best crispy hash browns in the area.

It was a fifteen mile ride in each direction. Uphill most of the way might have meant downhill going back. It was now their challenge to attempt to never backtrack on as many rides as possible. Back in their saddles, they had just come over the rise and past the county fairgrounds when suddenly the silence was shattered by sirens blaring. It was a two-alarm blaze. Claire had often wondered what these farms and farmhouses did in case of a fire. There they were, miles from towns, with no fire hydrants or any help at all. Throughout the summer, she kept noticing ponds close to the houses on properties outside of town. At first, she thought they were decorative -- a little swimming hole rather than a pool. They usually had a small dock, and often children and families played by the water. They even fished. Now it became perfectly clear what the ponds were really for, as the farmer had already begun pumping water to the fire that looked like it must have started in the kitchen, probably while making crispy hash browns. The fire trucks were quick to respond, taking over pumping precious water from the pond through the truck's high pressure hoses. The fire was brought under control swiftly, and the family was safe.

In this part of the country, if you saw something like this you stopped and helped. Ben was off his bicycle and heading to the house in an instant. Claire corralled the children and quickly took them across the road, away from the house, in case the propane tank behind the house ruptured. Their parents were both helping where they could to save their home.

Afterwards Ben could see the anguish on Claire's face. Putting his arm around her he said "It's alright, no one's hurt. The fire's out."

"What about the children? They could have lost everything today. They could have lost their parents and their home." Even she could tell she was unduly shaken up. The flashback of being quickly taken out of class then taken away, made her almost nauseous.

Chapter Twenty-Four

Matchmaking hadn't been one of her prior strengths, but this time it was working out nicely. Owing it all to Claire, for weeks, Liz and John had been seeing a lot of each other. A complete surprise to both of them, as neither had expected to find love again. Tonight was Sunday and the four were having dinner at Ben's. Claire cooked an amazing island feast. They had hearts of romaine with a creamy lime vinaigrette, black bean salad, sweet potato and squash mash, and grilled jerk chicken. They sat on the patio telling her about the area and how it had changed. They talked about what they had all done in their previous lives, and about Liz's house renovation. At this point, Liz asked Claire if she was free the following Wednesday and requested she come to the house early that morning in her oldest work clothes. Claire was amused, as she hadn't even thought of packing work clothes when she packed for the Ohio trip earlier in the spring.

Liz said, "Wear your oldest and grubbiest. I have the sledgehammers, safety goggles, and gloves. Just show up -- I need your help."

Liz's renovation was coming along slowly. The next line of attack was the old bathroom next to her bedroom. She explained they were tearing it down to the studs. Fortunately, the wall between that bathroom and her adjoining master bedroom was not a supporting wall. The door she planned to cut through the bathroom wall into her bedroom fit the room's layout perfectly. The plan was to enlarge the old bathroom by expanding into part of the adjacent bedroom. That bedroom would be sacrificed, becoming instead the enlarged master bath and spacious walk-in closet. The hallway doors to the bathroom and the other bedroom would be sealed and plastered over. Claire was so proud of her friend's architectural mastery.

Liz explained how they were going to do this. The girls stood there armed, wearing their bandanas, goggles, and old jeans. Claire thought they looked pretty good and snapped a couple of pictures. The only problem with all of this, Claire mentioned, was that she had never hit a thing. She never spanked her children. Never even hit a pillow after her divorce.

Liz's only comment to that was, "We need to toughen you up!" They took their first blows at the walls and nothing happened. The women looked at each other perplexed. Blow after blow delivered no visible impact. It was hard getting the job started. They kept it up, hammering and hammering. Their arms were already tired and sore and they burst out laughing at what wimps they were being. Determined, they thrust their sledgehammers harder still at the walls.

Finally, the walls slowly began to give way, to crack and chip. With more blows, more began to happen, and tiles began to splinter. For Liz, nearly fifty years of looking at this tile symbolized all the memories she had wrapped up in her old family home. Those memories began to loosen and chip away with the tile. Every year, each stage of her life had seen these walls, as she returned to visit in good times and in bad.

Then it began! The cracks spread like cobwebs throughout the walls, cracking and splintering into chards. The old plaster and tile began to crumble, seeming to want to come down. It fell in chunks and sections, as if helping the women as they blasted through. These walls were only a metaphor, as the other walls, too, began coming down – the ones the women had built up around themselves over all the years. Walls they did not know until now existed. They hammered through the tile, smashing down the walls.

Liz shouted out, "This one's for Congressman Maylor, for humiliating me in front of my colleagues! I left the firm because of him. And this one's for my first husband Tony, for the bonehead he was!" Claire was so lost in her own thoughts, until she heard muffled noises beside her and began listening in. She heard, "And this one's for my second husband Ron, for standing there like a wimp and letting me leave him!"

Claire felt she had to get in on this cathartic moment, so she gave a hard swing at James. *Hmm, that didn't feel necessary,* she thought, aware that she had finished processing him so many years ago. Taking a swing at her old lecherous neighbor Steve felt better. Then suddenly she was eight again, recalling feeling confused and lost. Another swing produced an unexpected emotional cry to her mother. "How dare you go and leave me! Why?" – *why did you make me grow up all on my own?* She felt angry, so angry, as tiles crashed down around her. Again and again Claire struck the wall. *It was so hard!* Then her anger subsided and changed to sadness and tears; deep sadness for not knowing her today, but finally accepting the loss. She forgave her too for leaving when she did.

The women didn't even hear each other as they called off people, incidents, moments, and the hurts they had felt in their lives. This was the confessional, and both knew that neither would betray the other. Then Claire shouted out, "And." Liz became still as Claire said, "And this is for letting them! For not grieving them, or letting go of them sooner." Neither spoke as they kept tearing down the old walls. Exhausted by then; each made one final strike and the tile was completely down. They stood there for many moments, in still silence, as all the dust and debris came to settle.

All the heartaches had come up to see the light of day. Claire thought she had forgiven everyone a long time ago, but apparently not. In the process, she really forgave herself. Liz was so happy to do the same. This wasn't a solemn occasion at all. The women were energized, emboldened! Each knew they had made space that day. By releasing the old they had now made room for the new to enter in, going forward in their lives.

RECIPES

Grilled Jerk Chicken

1 whole chicken, cut up

A marinade of: 2 scallions, washed and chopped	2 cloves of garlic
2 tablespoons soy sauce	Juice of 1 lime
4 tablespoons olive oil	1½ inch piece of ginger, grated
1 tablespoon brown sugar	1 scant teaspoon cinnamon

1 habanero chile, seeded and chopped or 1 teaspoon (to taste) of hot sauce
½ teaspoon cumin
1 scant teaspoon dried mustard

½ teaspoon thyme	Pepper and salt

The marinade: In a small bowl mix together the brown sugar, cinnamon, cumin, dry mustard, thyme, salt, and pepper. In a re-sealable bag large enough for all of the chicken pieces -- mix together the remaining ingredients; the soy sauce, chopped scallions, garlic put through a garlic press, olive oil, the chili pepper, ginger, and lime juice. To this add the dry ingredients mixture. Mix well. Add the chicken pieces to the marinade. Marinate overnight.

Grill the chicken using some left over marinade during grilling. Serves 4.

Hearts of Romaine with Creamy Lime Vinaigrette

Romaine lettuce	3 scallions, chopped
5-6 radishes thinly sliced	¼ cup olive oil
Juice of 1 lime	Zest of ½ the lime
Salt and pepper to taste	½ cup crumbled gorgonzola cheese

Put dressing ingredients into a jar -- olive oil, lime juice, zest, salt, pepper and gorgonzola. Shake well and pour dressing over the salad. Remaining dressing can be stored up to 5 days.

Black Bean Salad

2 – 16 ounce cans of black beans, washed and drained

1 cup of flat leaf parsley, chopped

2 stalks of celery, chopped

Red onion, peeled and diced

1 red pepper, diced

½ cup of chopped cilantro

½ cup olive oil

½ lemon of grated zest

½ teaspoon Dijon mustard

½ teaspoon sea salt

1/3 teaspoon cumin

Scant ½ teaspoon pepper

Juice of 1 lemon

In a small bowl wisk together the dressing using olive oil, mustard, lemon zest, salt, pepper, cumin and lemon juice. In a large bowl combine the beans, celery, chopped red onion, red pepper, cilantro, and parsley. Pour the dressing over the bean mixture and mix well. Make at least two hours in advance.

Sweet Potato and Squash Mash

2 large sweet potatoes	3+ tablespoons butter, softened
1 acorn squash	Salt and pepper
½ teaspoon cinnamon	4-6 tablespoons orange juice, optional

Wash and prick the sweet potatoes and bake them in a 350 oven for one hour or until soft. At the same time cut the squash in half. Place the squash halves in a small oblong pan with 1 ½ inches of water in the pan. Bake the squash along with the sweet potatoes. Bake the squash for forty minutes or until soft. Scoop the sweet potato and, discarding the seeds, scoop the squash out of their shells and puree the mixture. Add butter, cinnamon, salt, and pepper to taste. Thin the mixture, if needed, with a few spoonfuls of orange juice. Serves 4.

Chapter Twenty-Five

The following Tuesday Charity came in with so much to tell Claire about Mat's family and all the gossip that was going around the table last Sunday. A fight even broke out. Jeff and Norma quickly left, thinking someone could get hurt. Suddenly, she stopped herself. "Well, if I didn't have all this drama to talk about, what would there be to talk about?" They looked at each other, "Good things too."

One of her ah-ha moments came when Claire asked what made her eat uncontrollably. "What is it? Is it sweet; like desserts, candy, cookies, chocolate, maybe ice cream, or hot fudge sauce? Or is it salty or spicy; like potato chips, nachos, maybe crackers, cheese, or pizza?" They sat there naming every food they could think of in the categories -- sweet, salty, or spicy, making them both hungrier by the minute. When they stopped, with a straight face, Claire said, "Well, cut that one out after two in the afternoon for now."

Charity chimed in, "Wait, are you kidding?"

"That's right, have dessert with breakfast if you have to, or have nachos and jalapenos for lunch. What's your food?

What makes you keep eating uncontrollably? Whatever it is, take it away for now."

This went on week after week, and now Charity was eating the vegetables grown in her own farm's fields. She chose light salad dressings and even the taste of freshly squeezed lemons and olive oil on her salads was making her taste buds come alive. As she ate less, she began tasting her food and enjoying it so much more than before. She slowed down mealtimes and engaged her senses. She breathed in the good aromas of her food and the good smells coming out of her kitchen. She stopped to notice she felt good after a nice meal and was coming to understand about having the relationship with food which she and Claire talked about. She liked the way she and food were now getting along!

She could not believe how she felt herself changing inside and out. She could honestly say she felt better and was feeling happier in her life again. She was checking in and noticing how she spoke internally and to others. She was even laughing more and getting on the floor to play with her grandchildren again. Her jeans were comfortable, big even, and she realized she had a waist once again.

She thought she was getting close to trying on some old jeans hanging in the closet. They were part of her next-size-down wardrobe, the clothes she hadn't worn in at least three years. Next to them hung the two and three sizes down wardrobe, and buried in the back of her closet she kept a secret stash, her size eights. Those clothes were old and out of style. Keeping two of her favorite dresses back there, she assured herself styles do come back around. They hung out of sight, but she knew they were there. Till now, they had only stood as a sad reminder.

She was walking around the reservoir four days a week and spent the time working on that meditating thing Claire had taught her. Encouraged, she kept at it. It was hard, but walking helped still her runaway thoughts. Something was working! She hadn't been weighed in months, only stepping on the scale at the doctor's office. Finding the old scale where she had hidden it away in the laundry room, she was ready to weigh herself again and stepped onto it.

Claire rushed to the door, hearing pounding and the door bell ringing repeatedly. Practically busting through the door, Charity exclaimed, "We're celebrating! I just got on the scale and it is official. I've lost nine pounds!" Both girls started dancing right there and high fiving. Charity was so proud of herself. "We are celebrating!" Claire said, opening a bottle of champagne. Charity had never had champagne in the middle of the day, and the bubbles tasted so good with the cheese and spinach phyllo pie, and salad they had for lunch that day. Claire toasted, "Here's to all your success, my friend, and all the success ahead of you."

As the girls chatted about the Center, Charity asked, "How did you get started in this school business? What made you do this; were you a teacher? I was a teacher. I only taught one year after Mat and I got married, then we had the kids."

Where did this focused passion for children come from? Claire thought. "Children need to be nurtured and loved. Schools alone can't always do it, families aren't always there, so the community needs to pitch in and work together. I've always been good at bringing people together. I started early. My mother died when I was eight."

Claire surprised even herself talking about this, and could see Charity shift uncomfortably in her chair. "Claire, I'm sorry, I had no idea!" Charity said.

"That was a long time ago. I was alone suddenly and needed to quickly come together with my new brothers, my new parents, whom I barely knew, and a new school too. Intuitively I must have felt that I had to be the one who needed to put forth the most effort to get us to all come together. Up until that time I only knew people in my hometown environment and lived in the security thinking we would be together forever. Isn't that how we think as children?" Claire said.

"I've always thought that way." Charity said.

Claire thought about that comment for a second. *Yeah, we're never separate; we're always part of a community.* "I grew up in a small town too, in rural Illinois. One day, without ever having the chance to say good-bye, I moved to a suburb of Chicago." Remembering she went on, "I suppose since then there has always been a hole in my heart. Organically, because of my past and trying to fill the sad place in me, I've always nurtured young people at the elementary school level. I'm passionate to not let any child feel left out!" Her voice noticeably trailed off, "Oh my goodness..." she suddenly paused, *Why didn't I see this before?* Practically under her breath she continued, "Probably because I felt estranged for so long myself. I had to be brave." She looked at Charity amazed by her discovery! "That isn't at all why I thought I started the schools. I've always thought it was because of my interest in children's education. My degree was in child psychology. I love watching children learn and grow and be their own beautiful, special souls. I thought I began the schools to put that purpose to good use and to help others."

"I didn't realize I was filling a personal void. I was the child who felt left out and who needed to be nurtured. I remember thinking I had to get over my mother being gone quickly, or no one would want me." *And I might die, too.* Claire was openly transfixed at this revelation.

Charity saw Claire differently from that day on. All she could say was, "You've done an amazing job. I'm so glad you came here." The subject comfortably changed and they discussed what Claire looked for when she hired someone to fill the managing director's position. She said she had some qualified candidates and was doing the final screenings.

After Charity left, Claire began cleaning up the kitchen and putting the food away while retracing what had just occurred. *Is this possible? Am I only now dealing with the grief? Impossible! And yet...* she thought. *Why has this never occurred to me before? It's so obvious! That's why the schools, why kids, why the ceaseless desire?* She had never before seen this as her mother's gift to her. Through tears of joy, this time, she knowingly said, "It finally makes sense. Thanks Mom." At once she noticed there was plenty of food and champagne left over. This called for a celebration -- tonight after cycling.

RECIPES

Cheese and Spinach Phyllo Pie

1 pound Phyllo pastry sheets	5 eggs
20 ounces cottage cheese	1 box frozen spinach
6 ounces of crumbled feta cheese	1/3 cup sparkling club soda
½ teaspoon sea salt	Pepper to taste
½ cup vegetable oil	

Keep the phyllo covered so it does not get dry while you are assembling the rest of the ingredients. Preheat the oven to 350 degrees.

Use fresh spinach or an easier way is to use a package of frozen spinach. Squeeze every drop of water out of it that you can. Chop the spinach. In a large bowl add the cottage cheese, crumble the feta, and add the chopped spinach. Add the eggs, salt and pepper, blend well, don't over mix. You don't need to add the club soda but it is the secret ingredient to making the cheese fluffier. Use either a 12 inch round or a 14 inch oblong pan. Drizzle the bottom of your pan liberally with oil. You don't want the phyllo to stick. Place a layer of phyllo sheets in the pan and let them drape over the sides. Spoon in a layer of the cheese mixture. Crinkle another layer of phyllo leaves and place them loosely on top of the cheese. Drizzle some oil on the phyllo, add another layer of cheese mixture. Crinkle several more leaves around the pan, creating another layer of phyllo sheets. Drizzle more oil. Follow with the rest of the cheese. Top the cheese with one more layer of phyllo leaves and bring the draped sheets up into the pan. Drizzle the remaining oil all over the top of the pie. Don't be afraid that you're using too much oil. Too little will make the pie stick to the pan.

Bake the pie for 1 hour and 20 minutes. It will be golden brown when you remove it. The important step now is to hold a cutting board or large knife against the pan and tip the pan to drain any oil. This step must be done as soon as you remove the pie from the oven.

Chapter Twenty-Six

Claire was feeling uneasy because September was fast approaching. There was not a lot of time before the beginning of the school year. Thank goodness this year the elementary school had its plumbing issues to repair. The town certainly had its troubles, and she also understood Ben had a serious public relations problem. So how could they make this a win-win for everyone; a situation benefiting the children, their families, the field workers, Ben, and the community at large? She and Ben spoke at length, and he had begun crafting a plan weeks before.

That summer he began to see the town through her eyes and, getting to know Norma and Jeff again, he was seeing the town through theirs as well. The children who attended the public school were in a wonderful position to gain a strong academic foundation and have fun learning. He had always helped children, but this way he could help even more.

Ben's concern in this small town, this bell jar, was people's perceptions. "Why do you care so much what other people think?" Claire asked.

"Come on, people in these small towns don't like us who come back with money after being gone for a long time. These people are proud. They'll tell you they've stuck it out here while the rest of us left, as if we abandoned the town. I know that sounds ridiculous to you, but that's how people here are. Bill and Yvonne, Liz, John, me, and others -- we can all help and do more if we were just accepted back without the distrust and hostility towards us," he said.

She thought about what he was saying and about people's perceptions she had run into in life, then spoke, "They discriminate because of misguided perceptions and their own fears. Time's passed, and in many ways they're afraid of you now. They feel they don't know you anymore, so they created their own misinformed stories. Much of the time our human reaction is to distrust or not accept whatever we don't know or understand. You left as a boy and returned a wealthy man. You built a large home and bought a lot of land in the county. Local people could be resentful. But that's their problem. They judged wrongly. You're a generous and caring man and would do what you could for Salinger."

The elementary, middle school, and high school were all situated at the midpoint of Maple Avenue, just south of the business district. Bob Fuhrman, Ben's realtor, had checked on a vacant property that had sat empty for about three years. There were no liens on the property and the taxes had been paid. This building was around the corner from the school. The back of the school grounds butted up against part of the property. It had been a 7-Eleven and gas station once, with an extra large area in the back for truck parking. For some unknown, fortuitous reason, the underground gas storage tanks had already been removed, filled in with sand and gravel, and the property repaved. Ben had already discussed the project with Carl Yost, who owned the outdoor furniture plant in town, which was staying put, right here in Salinger. Carl was in support of the project all the way, and gave the board $50,000 toward the property and build out. With that support Ben negotiated a long-term lease with an option to buy. Together they would lease the space and do the renovations to the building. As far as the Center's operating budgets were concerned, he would speak to Bill Klaussen regarding matching funds. That money had to be deposited into a separate escrow account. By doing this, they would help the Center build equity while it raised operating capital. Ben, Carl, and Bill had to be able to audit the books at any time so they could see the Center was raising enough money to support itself.

Ben had other stipulations, as well. During the summer, the Center would be operational as a drop-off day school for working parents, and migrant worker's children would be bussed to the Center daily. There was one more condition. Year round in the evenings, after the children went home, Alcoholics Anonymous and its affiliate programs would meet at the facility. Ben felt, if he was being put under a microscope, the people of Salinger had better look at themselves as well. Jobs were hard to find, but he would only hire people who he could trust to put in a full day's work.

The only thing still eluding Claire was who from the community would be the outreach person, whose responsibility it was to maintain the "Safe Schools Off-Campus Program" regulations. Claire asked Norma if she would volunteer and was quickly rejected. Did Norma know of anyone? Not off hand. She would have to wait and see what would transpire.

Charity had been perfectly content for years simply taking care of her family, working on church activities and projects, and throwing in her two-cents worth in wherever there was controversy in the community. More and more she was feeling a strong sense of obligation and compassion towards the people in her town. She thought about how blessed she was that her family members were all healthy. She was able to stay home with her children while they were growing up, and her husband always had a well-paying job. She wondered, *When did I start feeling so sorry for myself?* The joys of life had eluded her for so long she had forgotten how to be involved in life and how to listen to her heart speaking to her. *Funny this love and happiness thing of Claire's*, she thought. *It has a quick effect on everyone around her. I had forgotten how to love bigger.* Charity wanted to feel good all the time now and knew how to more and more.

"Happiness and peace of mind do have a ripple effect, and no ripple effect on the Earth is a small event. Just like throwing a rock in a pond and watching the waves stretch all the way across the pond, that's the way the Earth's energy is affected. People affect other people, and no one is too small or too insignificant to inspire change around them. We can all make a difference, and it starts right where we are. This is how we heal the planet," Claire had said. Charity remembered her saying this at one of their early lunches and had thought she was being strange at the time. Now she understood.

She was interested and wanted to know all she could about the Center. Asking one day if she could be involved, Claire directed her to Norma. It was time these two reconciled their differences, thought Claire, and she was delighted, of course, as there was still that one last position to be filled. Charity had been asking enough questions in recent weeks that Claire had been waiting, feeling eventually she would come forward. Claire believed she would make an outstanding outreach person for the Center. Charity could continue the fund-raising efforts and monitor internal school systems. She also knew Mat and Norma would not let her fail. Claire was getting close to hiring the managing director and would include Charity in all the ongoing work from now on. She was a dream come true for Claire as well. Personally investing herself in every Center, she was fierce for "her" children's welfare, wanting each labor of love to remain in good hands. Norma called that evening. She knew Charity had spoken with Claire regarding the position, and Norma gave her blessings.

In many ways, Charity thought, the Children's Center was her dream coming true. Admittedly, it had only just begun to manifest in her mind recently. Now she felt as if she cared more than ever before. She remembered how much she loved teaching when she and Mat first got married. And how she talked about all the things she could do for the people who worked at Nagel Farms. Then they started their family, and Charity kept putting her own ideas and dreams on hold. By not acknowledging or implementing any of her inspirations or desires, eventually they stopped coming to her, or maybe she just stopped hearing them. She hadn't even noticed. Now she felt the desire again. She was grateful for what was happening. She felt like a new person. Things just seemed to be falling into place.

A meeting was called for later in the week. Carl Yost attended, and Ben laid out their plan and proposal for renovating the building and housing the school. The board also officially welcomed Charity as their outreach and "Off-Campus" specialist. Norma had conducted a poll and the new name for the Center was "The Off-Campus Children's Center." Claire smiled; *It was a great name and was working all over the country.*

Claire was feeling restless. The project was under control and the Center was close to having a life of its own. This is where she usually made her exit.

Chapter Twenty-Seven

Time to go home. It's time to check on the house. Be with Lisa, visit the schools, there's the Big Brothers Big Sisters event. Claire could go on and on. Brad Wells and Joann Pierce worked as independent contractors for Claire and travelled extensively to the various schools around the country. It was time to call a meeting and bring them to Palm Beach for a couple of days. Joann covered the territory from Georgia to Washington, DC, and lived in Charlotte, North Carolina. Brad lived in Michigan and traveled the Midwest and Midsouth regions of the country. Claire decided there were lots of reasons not to stay in Ohio.

"I'm leaving tomorrow." Claire finally told Ben while they were out cycling. "I'll leave my car at the airport. I have a flight at noon."

"How long have you been planning this?" he asked.

"I've been putting off going back down for a couple of weeks. The schools can't run themselves. I have to get back and check on everything. I've never stayed away this long."

"When are you coming back? Are you coming back?" he asked.

"I'll probably be back in a couple of weeks." If someone were doing this to her she would be livid, she thought. Giving no warning she felt safer this way. After the ride Claire decided to go home and avoided Ben completely.

Back in Palm Beach she was quick to return to her over-scheduled way. "I'd like you to come to the house everyday Lisa." They worked daily from nine till nearly six. Several days while Lisa let herself in and worked, Claire left and visited the schools in West Palm, Coral Gables, Naples, and Orlando. These were the immediate vicinity schools within a three hour drive of her. In the evenings she accepted every invitation she received. She spoke to her children almost daily and made sure she was never alone until she went to bed exhausted at the end of the day.

"Something's going on with Mom." was the consensus among the three.

The first day Ben called five times. They talked as if everything was fine. The next day he called all day again, and the day after that too. Finally he said, "You haven't picked up the phone to call me. What's going on? What's going on with the Center here?"

"Everything is on schedule; Charity and Norma can liaison." said Claire

"Charity, oh really, you're just throwing her in," he said genuinely surprised by the decision.

"I've spent weeks talking to her about the Center. We talk daily, and she'll be working independently within weeks anyway." That was the way of their conversations through the next couple of days. Then the fighting ensued and even became personal. "Stop trying to control everything. You don't know where this could lead, and I don't either. I don't like your cooking. I just want some fried chicken and mashed potatoes sometimes." After that conversation he stepped back and waited for her to call. It was still too early in their relationship for Ben to say what he really felt, which was, "Come back!"

She thought about his cooking comment. As ridiculous as it sounded, why hadn't he said something sooner? *I just wanted to keep you healthy. I don't want to lose another person I care about.*

During the second week Lisa finally asked, "Why the crazy schedule? I thought you were taking some time off this summer? We've got everything under control here. I love having you back, but you can go anytime. Just let me know what to do and it'll be done. And my family will like seeing me around again."

Chapter Twenty-Eight

*C*laire realized she had not once made time to take a walk on the beach. Living here, and being within walking distance of the beach, she discovered long ago it was her great escape. Stepping in the sand made all the worries of the day go away and she could feel her heart open wide as she basked in the sun's rays and salt air. These walks had become almost sacred.

Today as she walked, she picked up a shell along the way, crouched down, and wrote her wishes in the sand. Then sat down and watched as the waves washed up on shore and took the words back to the ocean where she knew they were invisibly manifesting. She always thought she could not imagine living anywhere else again.

Walking back from the beach Claire recognized a familiar car in her driveway. Opening his car door David got out to greet her. "Perfect timing! You're wonderful to be here! I'm so happy to see you!" she said, throwing her muggy, sandy arms around him.

"I'm glad to be here too. I knew I'd find you here. I wanted to let you know, I'm going to check on the gallery now, and come back." He was glad to see his friend again.

Excited, she said, "I'll shower and clean up. Can you be back for dinner in about an hour?"

Returning soon after, "You've been missing in action and it was strange not to hear from you these past few days. By the way, that's a great dress. I love that color on you." David said, as they walked into the living room.

"Thanks, it felt good to do a little shopping again. And I know, I've meant to call. I've just been so busy. You missed it; we were a sponsor again this year for the Big Brothers Big Sisters event. I knew you had your hands full up north so I didn't call to remind you. When did you get in?" Claire said.

They caught up on the Chicago news and the news about David's parents. David added, "Justin sends his love and hopes we all get together again soon."

Claire had twenty questions for David avoiding any potential questions directed at her. Never discussing politics or the news, she even went into the state of the economy and jobs numbers. She told him about the school project in Nashville, Tennessee, which she was negotiating. She also told him about the completed Indianapolis project, the open house weekend, and the good possibility of opening another location there. "So, as you see, it was the perfect time to return home, for a while at least," she said, convincing herself.

"You left in kind of a hurry didn't you? I spoke with Ben. He called me to find out if you were alright. He's worried about you. He remembered the name of my company, Complete Systems AV, and called a couple of days ago. It took me a while to rearrange my schedule and get down here. I got in this morning."

It was already seven thirty, "Let's take this conversation into the kitchen. Are you hungry?" Claire pulled a pot of vichyssoise out of the fridge, made a salad, and piled a board high with a white bean dip, cheeses, smoked salmon, bread, grapes, pears and figs. It was fig season again. "And we have a fig tart for dessert. I made it for Lisa and me yesterday. She seems to think that I'm not needed here any longer and should return to Ohio."

"What about you? What do you think? Claire, it's your private business, but unless you have a reason not to want to be with this guy, I think he deserves a chance," David said.

"I think about him. Care about him. I find myself wanting to be with him and holding him. How can that possibly work? I live here and he prefers to be there," she said.

"You guys haven't talked about all of the logistics? I find that hard to believe. What is it really?" David persisted.

"I have a full life in every other way; maybe I'm not meant to have love in my life. It's probably better to end it now before we're both even more attached," she said.

"Is that what you want? No love. You can have that, if you want it that way. I'm your friend, and it's as clear to me as your dress is blue. You're self-sabotaging your happiness." After an uncomfortable silence he asked, "What fulfills you?"

"You know me -- I love the schools, the kids. I love to help people, and be there for my friends and my family," she answered.

"That's why I think you're scared and self-sabotaging your happiness. You find it easier to give and you shut the door on receiving from anyone. When it gets too close and your deepest emotions are touched, you -- well, it looks to me like you run away. You can't handle someone just loving you."

"That's cruel!" she objected. "Can we really have happiness in all the parts of our lives? I'm good in so many areas, thank you for pointing that out, but I don't know if we can have it all."

"You can't if you don't believe you can. There's no difference in the way you embrace your work. You do it with love. The way you embrace me, your children, and others -- you don't judge us, you love us unconditionally. Your personal happiness is no different. Keep that same love there. You're not a different person in different areas of your life. Live your love in every part of your life. Starting with you! That means no fear, no judgment, no self-sabotaging, and when you do, forgive yourself, stop being so hard on yourself. You're human like the rest of us; we're all growing." Then he said, "Like me," as he patted his belly. "Mmm, this is so good!" They were just starting dessert and coffee.

"You're so right," she contemplated as something revealed itself suddenly. "I'm reminding myself of Charity, the woman I sometimes speak of from Ohio. It's so obvious when I see those ah-ha moments on her face -- when something makes perfect sense to her and locks in." They continued talking, till he checked the time. "When am I going to see you again?" she asked.

As David got up to leave he said, "Probably not again 'til the fall."

Claire began cleaning up the kitchen. *What's really going on?* She thought as her emotions welled up. She could have stopped them here and overridden them; instead she listened, listened hard but she felt stuck. So she thought about it again, *What's really going on?* This time she listened with her heart to sense how she was feeling. *I'm angry because I'm even feeling this way. I want a relationship and yet I'm saying I don't need anything else in my life. I'm frustrated, why is this so hard? Why am I not making space for this man to*

151

come in? What's the deeper emotion? Claire felt her stomach tighten, *I'm afraid! Why? I'm afraid to be left alone again, afraid of the risk of having my heart broken again. And I'm sad too, because I keep making excuses saying it's alright for me to be sitting on the sidelines; that not jumping into this relationship and enjoying My life, are somehow acceptable.*

She could feel there was still more, something deeper, something she didn't want to touch. *Come on, show myself some compassion here!* She placed her hands on her chest and felt her heart opening. Gently she swung the doorway to her heart inward and felt her heart open even more. It was hard at first. It felt almost as if she wasn't sure it was safe. She swung the door inside still wider -- letting in the light, and could immediately feel the warmth, and love, and security that were always there. She stayed like this and took several deep breaths – she didn't want to leave the experience yet, knowing that too often we walk away from feeling good too quickly, denying ourselves the full depth and joy of the moment. She felt sympathetic toward herself because it always came back to haunt her when the stakes were high -- she always unconsciously found a way to behave like the lost little girl she remembered. "Ok, I'm ready to heal from this; to let go of it."

What an epiphany! Recognizing the significance of what had just occurred she was at once grateful. *Thank you for exposing what I couldn't see before. Thank you for David, for Ben, that crazy place in Ohio, and for what I'm about to say.*

Checking her watch it wasn't too late to call. "Ben, it's me." Making small talk at first and gauging the temperature of their conversation, she said, "I can't not be together. I've tried to see it every way, and I keep coming back to the truth: I want to be there with you."

RECIPES

Vichyssoise

1 pound of potatoes or 2 large baking potatoes, peeled
and cut in small chunks

3 large leeks

3 tablespoons of butter

Generous sprinkling of salt
and white pepper

6 cups of chicken stock

¾ cup half and half

Keep peeled and cut potatoes in cold water while cleaning
and chopping the leeks. Wash the leeks and discard the green
bottoms. Slice the leeks vertically down the center to wash
them well. Chop the leeks, drain the potatoes and place them
in a saucepan with the butter and a generous sprinkling of
salt and pepper. Sauté on medium heat. Sweat the leeks, don't
let them brown. Add the chicken stock, bring to a boil then
simmer for 1 hour. Turn off the stove and soon after puree
the soup in batches. Add the half and half to the pureed soup.
Refrigerate and serve cold as vichyssoise. Also delicious hot.

White Bean Dip

1 fifteen ounce can of Cannelli or Great Northern beans
1 clove of garlic   3 tablespoons olive oil
1 teaspoon white wine vinegar   1/3 teaspoon cumin
½ teaspoon sea salt   Black pepper
A little cayenne pepper   Juice of ½ lemon

Wash and drain the beans and pulse in your food processor. Add the garlic in thick slices. Add the olive oil and vinegar. Process for one minute. Now add the cumin, salt, pepper, cayenne, and lemon juice. Continue pureeing for another minute. The dip will be velvety in texture. Garnish with chopped flat leaf parsley and pine nuts.

Fig Tart

2 cups flour	¼ teaspoon salt
2 tablespoons sugar	1½ sticks cold butter
1 egg	2 tablespoons cold water
A container of mission figs, in season	3 ounce marzipan bar
1 tablespoon butter	1/3 cup sugar
¼ cup plum jam	

Preheat the oven to 425 degrees. In a food processor, make the tart pastry by combining the flour, salt, and sugar. Cut the butter into small pieces and add. Continue pulsing. Add the egg and water; blend until the pastry pulls away from the sides. Empty the pastry onto a sheet of wax paper and form it into a ball. Wrap it in the wax paper and chill for 1 hour or more. Remove from the fridge and roll it out, on a floured surface, to ¼ inch thick. Press the dough into a removable bottom tart pan. I can never get it to roll out well. Pressing it in is a perfect alternative. Place the pan on top of a cookie sheet in the oven. Place a sheet of parchment paper on the dough and cover the bottom with dried beans to keep the pastry shell even. Bake for 10 minutes. Remove the parchment paper and beans and bake 2 minutes more.

Wash and cut the ends off the figs and cut each into thin wedges. In a skillet, heat the butter and add the figs and sprinkle with 2 tablespoons of sugar. Glaze and cook for 5+ minutes. Remove from heat. Chop the marzipan and scatter it around the bottom of the tart shell. Arrange the figs on top and sprinkle with remaining sugar. Bake at 375 for 45 minutes, or until pastry is golden brown. Heat the plum jam, strain and spoon over the tart. Let cool so jam sets.

Chapter Twenty-Nine

*C*laire had been back a week. All tension, uncomfortable feelings, and mistrust between them had evaporated. Early Saturday morning, the day of the fair, they drove to the town of Platt, Ohio. Ben and Claire went to the Amish auction expressly to pick out five beautiful quilts. The pretty Amish woman sold them for two hundred dollars each. Claire recognized her immediately as they walked up to the stand. She passed this woman's home every time she drove out of town going east, and often wondered about her and what her life must be like. Whenever Claire came over the hill, she hoped to see her in the garden. She had a little boy who looked like he was four. He ran around the yard playing with his dog while she weeded the garden and picked fresh vegetables. She stood tall and willowy. Her complexion showed she had gotten a touch of sun. She always walked barefoot and wore the same dress and bonnet. Claire watched this woman, who must have been a young girl not long ago, mature and become radiant this summer.

They were donating these quilts for the raffle. Chances were forty dollars each and the winner could have the quilt of his or her choice. All proceeds went to build the new playground at the Children's Center.

Charity had been working on the Ellis County Fair committee at church. She, Norma, and their other sister-in-laws, Barb and Cathy, had spent all spring and summer planning the event. Now Charity was coming to them and the church board with a change in plans. She was asking them to change the theme of their booth this year, and asking if they would share their booth with the Children's Center. All the booths had already been assigned and paid for since last March. This was the only hope of spreading the word and raising money for the Center. Jeff was on the church board, and with his persuasion, they voted unanimously to share the booth. Charity's daughter Pam got involved, too. She called all the vendors asking if they would put a large jar in their booths with a sign requesting people donate their change. Pam and her husband were going to deliver the jars Thursday night before the fair. They were thrilled that every vendor agreed. It felt as if the whole county was putting energy into this project before there had even been an official announcement.

On the Friday before the fair, the front page of the Salinger Post ran a feature article about the scope of the project, and the means by which the town intended to pay for the new "Off-Campus Children's Center." There was going to be before and after-school child care even with the school's deep budget cuts! It was announced the school was donating the classroom and office furniture. (The school board was replacing everything that sustained damage from the water main break, and they had new furniture on order.) There was going to be a big new playground in the back. It was reported this weekend at the Ellis County Fair people should come out and support the project generously so the kids could start school the day after Labor Day with a brand new after-school program and playground. There would also be a signup sheet at the Merryvale Christian Church fair booth to volunteer to help build the playground on the Saturday before Labor Day, lunch included.

Claire suggested offering lunch all day. Charity said no to that immediately, warning all the money raised would go to feeding everyone and half the town would show up just for lunch.

They were on their way to making the playground a reality. Jeff and Norma donated the thousand dollar deposit for the playground equipment. Mr. Huffmeyer, the Amish man down the road from Nagel Farms, had already ordered the lumber and parts, and had begun construction. He promised delivery on the setup day at 6:30 a.m.

People from all over the county came to the fair. Not as many people were vacationing far from home, given the state of the economy, so the fair was packed. All the booths were busy the entire weekend. And every booth prominently displayed a Children's Center jar. People could be seen all over the fairgrounds stuffing their change and dollar bills into the jars. Charity walked around the fair several times during the weekend emptying the jars as they filled up. Jimmy Nagel, a pig farmer who was Mat's second cousin, gave Charity a check for five hundred dollars and said, "Give me twelve chances on a quilt." Everyone was feeling generous, and many of the vendors were having such a profitable fair this year they stopped Charity and asked her to call on Monday, after the fair, so they could make their donations.

Claire and Ben arrived around noon, going straight to Jimmy's for the best sausages and bratwurst she had ever tasted. Jimmy loved talking to all the people, and every year he took a booth. He butchered one of his hogs, and prior to the event he made up a hundred pounds of sausages. He and his son sold out every year. Too busy to stop and talk, he called out to Ben that he had just made a donation and thanked Ben for everything he was doing.

158

Claire and Ben parted ways after lunch. He was on his way to watch the livestock judging and was she sure she did not want to come along. He was ready to give her a head full of farm animal facts. She assured him she would have loved to but was scheduled to work in the church booth from one to five. The smells of funnel cakes, fried chicken, and dirty diapers sounded a lot better to her than those of livestock on this ninety degree Ohio day.

Charity was so happy to see Claire again and ran up to give her a big hug. "Welcome back girlfriend." At the same time, Liz and John came by the booth with John's ten-year-old nephew, Seth. Claire had been wanting to introduce them to Charity. It turned out that Mat's younger brother Bruce had been in the same class as Liz. John and Mat had been classmates too. Liz and John each pledged a thousand dollars for the Center, receiving fifty chances in the raffle. Liz was saying she wanted a handmade quilt for the new sunroom that was nearly finished. Claire could see a little drywall spec hanging from her hair. Picking it out gently, the two of them burst out laughing as they remembered their demolition day. John voiced, "I was so impressed with the great job you girls did tearing out the old bathroom walls! I finished breaking apart the floor the same weekend." The ladies winked at each other and thought, *Was it as good for him as it was for us?*

Claire asked, "Are you coming back for the dinner dance this evening?" They replied yes, and decided they would all sit together.

High school seniors whose parents knew about the internships, were stopping by to ask Mrs. Nagel when they could interview or sign up to work at the Center. They wanted her to know how excited they were. Was it true that they could get college credits?

Claire got a ride home as Ben had left the fair hours before her. Showering off the dust and grime, she managed to close her eyes for twenty minutes, and then got ready for the evening. This was another first, she thought, never having been to a county fair dance before.

There wasn't a cloud in the sky that night and the moon and stars shone a spotlight down on the party. It was a perfect eighty degree night and there were ten people at their table. Claire thought how wonderful it was to see Charity and Norma being best friends again. When hearing Liz was back in town, Bruce, Mat's younger brother, and his wife Barb joined the table. Everyone was having a great time laughing and talking together, dancing and even square dancing. Claire hadn't square danced since Miss Smith's seventh grade gym class. The DJ was from Columbus and was having fun with the crowd. The rural stereotyping was so evident to Claire, but no one else seemed to notice or care. Everyone was having fun wherever she looked. After the fireworks, they all walked back to their cars and drove home. On the way back, Ben said, "This was the best county fair I've been to since I was fourteen. That's when Missy Perkins kissed me behind the Ferris wheel." Claire laughed. She was definitely a million miles from home and thought, *You just can't make this stuff up!*

Chapter Thirty

*T*uesday after the fair Charity marched into Claire's calling out loudly, "I knew it, I knew it, I knew it! You and Ben are together. I could see it at the fair. You're perfect for each other! They told me in the beginning of the summer you weren't. I wasn't fooled!"

Lunches were never the same, and this morning Claire stuffed light green sweet banana peppers with brown rice, lentils, and ground beef. The peppers were baked in a light tomato broth, and the girls dipped their bread and sipped iced tea while they worked. Charity continued to come on Tuesdays, and they added Wednesdays and Thursdays since there was much for her to learn. Being Tuesday, what Charity really wanted to know was: what pearl of wisdom Claire would come up with this week?

This one was a doozy! "Step in front of the mirror naked. Look at how beautiful your body is. Run your hand up your leg. Feel your thigh. Feel the curve of your waist and the bump of your belly. Look at yourself, and touch your beautiful, full breasts."

"Claire! You are so weird!"

"Why not, it connects you with your body. We need to honor and love our bodies. They take us from here to there. They interact with people, bringing us satisfaction; whether you're with Mat, me, or your grandchildren. It is self-healing and regenerative to love and honor yourself. You are a beautiful woman."

"I've never done that!" They laughed and all Charity could say as she blushed was, "Here goes!"

Later in the week she was eating a hot fudge sundae for dessert one evening. It was her reward, having had a very hard day. She couldn't remember when the last time was she had eaten dessert, but this was a day to go off and splurge. As she ate mechanically, the way she used to eat a hot fudge sundae, suddenly she got a feeling in the pit of her stomach telling her she wasn't even hungry for it. She was eating because it was what she had always done in the past when she had a very tough day.

These days she was taking herself far less seriously as well, and thought she would try something new out on Mat. With no warning, she picked some of the hot fudge up from her bowl and smooshed it around her mouth, like a clown face, and then went over and gave him a big hot fudge kiss. They both laughed and she smeared some on his face, too. He went along with it. "What's gotten into you? You never act like this."

"Maybe I should more often," she purred. That night, she came to bed not wearing anything and found Mat waiting for her. She couldn't remember when their love felt so good. She could feel again, and she knew Mat felt her relax and move with him for the first time in a long time. They didn't speak afterwards, but he held her like he used to. She woke the next morning, forgetting she had come to bed without her nightgown, and smiled, knowing she was beautiful and sexy.

Early on Claire said one wish or one desire is never enough and that Charity should just keep coming up with desires – then let them go; that our desires, happiness, and pleasures are found all around us. We just needed to be open to receive them. One of Charity's desires was for her and her husband to get their marriage back, and it was working.

RECIPES

Stuffed Sweet Peppers

6 sweet cubanelle peppers   1 pound ground sirloin
1 small onion, peeled and chopped 1 large tomato
Olive oil   ½ cup lentils
¾ cup brown rice   ¼ teaspoon pepper
1 – 8 oz can of tomato sauce   ½ teaspoon sea salt
1½ cups of water

The Roux:

3 tablespoons olive oil   2 tablespoons sweet paprika
2 tablespoons flour

Preheat the oven to 350 degrees. Wash and gently cut the tops off the peppers and remove the seeds. In a 10" skillet sauté the onions in a little olive oil. Add the ground beef, salt and pepper. Sauté until the meat is browned. Drain the excess grease from the pan. Add the brown rice and lentils. Blend well. Gently stuff the peppers with the meat mixture and arrange them lying down in a roasting pan. Cut the tomato in 6ths and put a piece of tomato inside each pepper to close the end. In a separate bowl mix the tomato sauce and 1 cup of water. Pour over the peppers. The peppers should be almost submerged in the sauce mixture. Add the rest of the water if more liquid is needed. Place the roaster in the oven and bake for 45 minutes. Prepare the roux by heating 3 tablespoons of oil in a small pan. When oil is hot add the flour and paprika. Fry the mixture, being careful not to burn the flour. Remove the roaster of peppers from the oven and add the roux in spoonfuls into the sauce and blend. The roux will thicken the broth. Return the roaster to the oven and bake an additional 45 minutes. Serves 4.

Chapter Thirty-One

$\mathcal{A}$bout six miles from the farm they saw another truck parked in a driveway. Claire was noticing them now, too, and was aware of the concern on Ben's face.

A beautiful evening ride through farm country engaged the senses. Claire's mind was fully immersed on another plane as she became lost in thought. She had told David, "Being outside in the wide open space with your heart rate up and cycling at your own pace creates a perfect environment to practice living with an open heart; if you just get out of your own way and experience it."

Settling into her cadence she began thinking about those weeks before, the way in her mind – in her fear, she had justified stepping away from this remarkable time in her life. She had been unwilling to receive the good she was being presented with. *It takes living with an open heart to be open to receiving. Almost literally, it feels like a doorway exists to your heart. It can be a beautiful French door or inviting gate.* She visualized, *which you have the choice to open -- opening it inward, showing love and compassion for yourself, or being swung out, giving and sharing your love and energy with the rest of your world.* Heart open to her, Claire visualized standing in a beautiful, sunny garden with a refreshing gentle spring; which when it swung out led to an expanse that opened to a vast, sunny, all-encompassing landscape with no end.

Several years before Claire had heard a speaker who influenced the way she decided to live her life going forward. She put living with an open heart to the test and over time discovered her life worked better when she personified love. She thought, *Walking with an open heart requires practice in a safe environment. Much like practicing a musical instrument, or public speaking, getting better or bolder does not come without repetition. It's easy to say open your heart, but it may be new, unfamiliar – so it takes courage, commitment, and some getting used to. Remaining heart-centered means coming from love instead of fear. As adults it's a choice we make, it does not come naturally. Choosing to think from love, and saying yes instead of no is practicing accepting instead of judging. Being irritated, resisting, evading, criticizing, or arguing are all expressions and actions of saying no.*

She and Ben were riding past the old abandoned stone house. It sat back off the road nearly unnoticeable, surrounded by a neglected overgrown hedge. Intrigued, Claire had stopped earlier in the summer and photographed it. You could not come close as the doors and windows were shrouded by thick thorny branches and spinney vines which made it impossible for any intruder to satisfy their curiosity. This evening the sky cast a light which made it look as if the house beckoned you to come closer and try once more. Distracted for a while Claire returned to her train of thought. *Choosing love or keeping an open heart simply means being generous when we don't have to be. It is being patient. Not giving in and certainly not being a martyr. Instead, it is being true to yourself with your boundaries intact. And why we need to practice is because where we really need this confidence to walk with an open heart is in our relationships, as we react to and respond to those around us.*

They were making their way up a hill. Her mind shifted to feeling her body fueling and pumping, engaging her muscles. Feeling the lactic acid building made her muscles burn. Then it calmed down, eventually dissipating. It felt good feeling her body release toxins while engaging the land with her senses, thoughts, actions, her feelings, and energy. Deciding to change the view, she shot out ahead of Ben.

Wind gusts came from the north as they rode in a southeasterly direction. Everything around them felt still. Neither spoke, not wanting to disturb the peaceful quiet. It was not silent by any means; instead, it was an evening when you heard a rustling wind whisper through the fields. An echoing *whhhooshsh* was heard in every direction one turned to listen. The wind gave each direction a distinct quality of sound and the rhythmic sway with which it engaged the fields kicked up the sensual smells of the grass and plants, mixing them with the earth's primal scent.

They were on their way back home after a late ride. Already 7:30 p.m., the sun had dropped low in the sky. Up ahead, a once white barn strikingly glistened in the evening light. The way the sun hit the roofline, and the angle at which the sunlight streamed and found a hole in the roof, made the whole barn light up from within. Heaven had lit a candle inside, and you could see the luminescence between the deteriorated boards. Soft light pierced through every few inches, every few feet, making the faded barn appear nearly translucent against the gray evening sky. Riding toward it from a distance, the colors and the heat of the day rising made it waver to the eye, like a mirage. Sitting off by itself about fifty feet away from a newer, better-built barn, it had been abandoned and forgotten a long time ago. Now it stood as a safe haven for mice, groundhogs, and birds, who built their nests and burrows away from the cold and rain. Riding past, a roar lifted! The shattered silence startled both cyclists. Three large hawks took off at eye level from behind the barn, soaring up into the sky. They rode with Claire and Ben. Of course they were faster, but twice they doubled back and flew above, as curious about the humans as Claire was about them.

Chapter Thirty-Two

At lunch, Claire described prosperity consciousness. "It's not limited to just how much money we have or make, or to what we can afford to buy ourselves. That's an important piece, but it's not all. It's also allowing yourself to receive the good, the grace around you. You saw me shut myself off not willing to receive a love I've wished for. Each person is perfect and completely worthy of the best they can imagine for themselves. That never changes; only their relationship to knowing it and to knowing who they are continues to evolve, and that's prosperity consciousness. It begins inside."

Charity said, "Some of these words you use, I don't understand them. But I watched you almost blow it, and it would have been no one's fault but yours."

"Ok, I'm guilty. Glad I could show you what I'm talking about." They both laughed and she went on, "It's activated when we let the joyful feelings inside express and not block them. When you are aware and focused on appreciating your life; you are grateful for and happy with what you already have. You know what I mean. You've been describing it lately."

By keeping her attention more closely focused on herself, Charity said, "I'm watching myself, sort of. I'm more aware of myself and what I'm doing and thinking during my day, not only reacting to whatever's happening. Well, at least I can do it some of the time. I hear myself talking to myself. If I don't like what I hear, I cancel, cancel! Some days I feel like a different person inside, bursting with love and I'm happy, and nobody made me that way but me. I love those days! I want to keep having them! I remember the question you asked – 'what do I want?' I want to be happy. I like having that peaceful feeling when I can."

"Now you're becoming aware of being aware," Claire smiled.

She had lost twenty-four pounds so far. Norma couldn't believe it. Cathy wasn't speaking to her husband Jake, Mat's other brother, because he wanted her to lose weight, too. Some asked if she was sick, while others told her how wonderful she was looking. Charity thought back to the beginning of the summer and felt so much had changed. She thought of quitting many times, choosing to stay content within her misery and discomfort because it was familiar. "I wanted to walk away from you so many times. Why should you be nice to me? What did you want from me? You were all the things I wasn't. But, you didn't seem to think that way and I felt like you really cared about me. You were there for me."

"I saw how fabulous you really are. I wanted you to see it too. You empowered yourself. It was all your doing. Something in you decided to take the chance and make a change. That took enormous courage to stick with it, and trust in yourself." Claire said. "And you gave me something special too, your friendship."

Charity was catching herself now before she spoke with family, neighbors, or friends. She had never before noticed complaining and criticizing was what she and her friends did. Now, after a few months of paying attention, all of this contrast was becoming confusing and just did not feel good any longer. She felt a tightening in the middle of her stomach as soon as she said something harsh. She often thought Claire used those words "how things feel" much too often. The more Charity slowed down and experienced how a situation was feeling, she came to understand she had a choice to make. She could respond the way she always had in the past, or she could change the way she thought and the way she answered. Sure, she still became angry and lost her temper, but it was happening far less. No matter how Charity's mother provoked her, she could not get Charity to fight back anymore. No matter how frustrated she became with the challenges of every day -- she felt less overwhelmed and more at peace. This was all still a mystery to her, and for now, she was fine with that.

Claire brought out a pad of paper the following Tuesday over lunch and said, "Make a list of everything and everybody who has bothered you, has offended or hurt you in the past. Think of everyone you need to forgive. Then on the other side of the paper, write down the things you have done or said to others for which you need to forgive yourself. Forgive everyone for everything, including you. Write them all down and burn the list."

That weekend, Charity and Mat were having all the kids over. Even Melissa was home from Chicago for a week with Brad and their two little ones. "Let's invite Ben and Claire to dinner Sunday night when the kids are all here," Charity suggested. They were having hotdogs and burgers on the grill, and Mat brought home a couple of dozen ears of corn. Dessert would be a s'mores marshmallow roast. Claire saved the surprise. S'mores around a campfire was one of Ben's favorite desserts.

Being a cool evening, the campfire kept them perfectly warm. The three-quarter moon lit up the sky. Claire observed how cute it was watching the little children climbing all over the men who were attentively helping them make their gooey s'mores. The girls cleaned up the dishes while the guys kept the children busy. The young husbands knew being together were special, precious moments for the sisters.

Charity went inside and brought out her folded paper. Claire brought hers along, just in case, and pulled it out of her pocket. They did not plan this ahead of time but were both ready. With a silent ritual, they simply threw the papers into the fire. Going up in flames, sparks carried the ashes away, taking with them all of the past; all of the hurts, the misunderstandings, everyone they had to forgive -- and yes, especially themselves. Ben and Mat looked at each other, and the grandchildren looked up at Grandpa puzzled. Mat said to the kids, "Your Grandma's been acting funny lately." And he smiled at her.

Chapter Thirty-Three

*C*harity picked up Norma, since she was already in her neighborhood delivering the last of the raffled quilts to Mrs. Hammond, who owned the dry cleaners in town. Jimmy had won one and told Charity it was a gift to his daughter-in-law, because every year he took away her husband to work at the fair. Liz picked out the quilt she wanted, and John won one, too. A family in Cleveland won the last quilt, and they had already driven over and picked it up.

It was just a few days before Labor Day weekend and Claire, Charity, and Norma were going through the list of last-minute details needing to be addressed. They were going down the list of guests invited to attend the ribbon-cutting and dedication ceremony, making sure no one who had been generous in helping bring the "Off-Campus Children's Center" to fruition was left out. Also, they made sure any person or business which could help in the future was also an invited guest. Every friend of the Center was a valued patron from now on and Charity understood her role in keeping the community closely aligned with the Center. Claire also suggested Salinger had a resource they had never fully accepted and welcomed back. Expatriates like Ben, John, Liz, and the Klaussens were certainly out there. Whether through recollections of childhood or just desiring to donate wherever they could; giving back, and contributing to the town enhanced how expats felt, and strengthened their commitment to the area. All they wanted in return was to be acknowledged like every other citizen, wanting to feel like a part of the community again. It was all part of choosing to return to their roots.

The board met at the Center later that day to do a walk-through of the newly renovated facility and ran through the schedule of events. Construction was complete, and the building was fully furnished, ready for guests to take the official tour. Knowing the building on the site would be big enough to house both classrooms and offices without need for additional build out, Ben had felt confident construction would be completed in time.

Marge Basset from right there in Salinger was hired as the managing director, and four college juniors were scheduled to begin internships on the first day of school -- two of which Claire was happy to report were Amish from the area and were education students at Bowling Green State University. Several high school seniors signed up to walk children over after school by way of the attached school yard and others were playground supervisors. Claire's parting words to the board were, "You've done it. The whole town, everyone, came together on this project and look what you've created! Congratulations."

On Thursday, Charity and Claire went shopping in Cleveland. This time it was Claire's turn to pick where they would shop. It was finally time for Charity to buy a new wardrobe. She had been putting it off far too long because she was still losing weight. With her new position in the community, it was now time to pick out a few new clothes. Representing the "Off-Campus Children's Center" was a new personal best for her. While Charity was in the dressing room

Claire brought clothes in for her to try and asked, "How many pounds did you lose this summer?"

Proudly responding Charity said, "Twenty-seven in four months!" As they were walking out of the store, Claire gave her a big hug. They continued to clothes shop for Charity, and then did some food shopping for Claire. Coming to the city almost always included a gallery visit and gourmet grocery stops. Not making it to a gallery this day was a foregone conclusion, but Claire could not miss the opportunity to stock up on good olives, cheeses, spices, wines, fish, and homemade cookies from Little Italy.

Saturday Mat and Jeff's volunteers would come to erect the new playground in the back of the Center. The rear of the building was large enough for the playground, still leaving plenty of room to bring out folding tables in the summer for students to eat their lunches and work on projects outside. On Friday, Charity and her committee bought all the food to make lunch for the volunteers. The fund-raising efforts just at the county fair had brought in enough donations to build the playground and escrow monthly expenses for at least the first nine months. Claire had a formula for keeping expenses manageable. As long as the non-profit Centers followed the budget guidelines, they would not get themselves into trouble.

Saturday morning at 6:30 a.m. Mr. Huffmeyer, who had built the sturdy playground equipment, met Jeff, Mat, and three of the volunteers at the Center to unload the truck. They set the playground parts in place, studied the plans, and were ready for the 8 a.m. start. Eighteen volunteers had signed up to build the playground structure. Then four more were coming after 3:00 p.m. to spread mulch all around the encasement. Ben had told a few of his migrant workers their children would have a good school to attend when they returned to the farm next summer, and the men wanted to show their appreciation. Right after their working day was over, they drove in to help. The mulch and railway ties arrived as a last minute donation from Frank's Garden Center.

Just after seven that morning, Charity arrived with thermoses of hot coffee for the men. Her lunch staff would not be there until eleven, so she was going back home for a while. Volunteers began slowly arriving, and there was hot coffee waiting. Right at eight the work began, and the people of Salinger began to pitch in. Twenty-five volunteers ultimately showed up to work and a dozen more watched. As they worked, cars passing by honked their horns and drivers threw change into colorful children's sandbox buckets that volunteers held out as cars stopped at the traffic light. Everyone seemed to be caught up in the excitement. The Post's reporters were there snapping pictures and interviewing anyone they could. The Boy Scout Troup sold lemonade and the Girl Scouts had a bake sale. Volunteers worked diligently and the playground stood erected by 2:30 that afternoon.

Then they all sat down to lunch. As the landscape team arrived, they joined in, and a bond was struck that had not taken place in this town since Ben, Mat, and Jeff's parents talked about how people pitched in to help, making it a better community. The Center was now finished and the last pieces were put into place. Somehow, or maybe just because human nature made it so, this town had become fragmented and was weaker for it. Parallel groups existed side by side yet rarely interacted: town's residents, expats, Amish, and migrant workers all lived their separate lives in this small twenty mile radius. The Center was bringing them together to address a common goal.

Sunday was a day of well-deserved rest, and when Monday came, the dream that began in April became a reality. All the officials and guests came to tour the new Center and attend the ribbon-cutting ceremony. Everything went as planned. After the tour, they all walked outside to the makeshift stage area. Claire sat in the front row with some of the others whom she had met on the first day. Mat sat next to her. Next to him sat Franklin and his wife. He had done all of the legal work required for the Center. He had also made sure that all necessary permits were expeditiously issued, and final inspections had gone smoothly. Dr. Smith and his wife made a very generous donation, and assured the board they would be long-term sponsors and advocates. They sat on the other side of Claire, and she was meeting his wife, Sally, for the first time. Right behind her sat Carl and Jane Yost. In front of the audience stood the Mayor, Ben, as the Center's Board Chairman, Norma, the representative of the Salinger School Board, and Charity, as community liaison. Right behind them were Jeff and the other city council members, and Mrs. Basset, the Center's managing director. In his speech, Mayor Brown used the best analogy local people could relate to, that of a harvest. He said, "People in Salinger make their living by understanding the land and seasons. The seeds we sowed in early spring are being harvested here today. The children are the precious seeds of the future for this deserving community. Thanks to all the people here who have made their lasting contribution in good faith, these cherished seeds will grow and continue to enrich our town."

The ceremony was kept brief and a time capsule was placed in the building's cornerstone. The Mayor, Ben, Norma and Charity cut the ribbon. The Post was quick to snap their picture. Applauses came from the audience and the ceremony was over. Everyone congratulated one another. Charity looked beautiful in her new dress and Mat came over and told her so. Norma looked relieved. The community had placed their trust in her, and she had accomplished the mission. She came up to Claire and gave her a hug, and shook her hand, like she did in the driveway the first day Claire arrived. Everyone was shaking hands and congratulating one another all the way to their cars. Driving home Claire thought about how during these recent weeks she had watched Ben receive his crash course in civics, while Charity was receiving hers in non-profit work. Grateful, she recognized that a lot had changed in her this summer too.

The next day school started, and Salinger had its "Off-Campus Children's Center." Claire woke up and went straight to get the paper. Before Ben left in the mornings, he always brought the newspaper in. She wanted to see the article about the ribbon cutting and how The Post had reported on the school. Whenever possible, she kept all articles about the schools for her business files.

Sharing the front page with the Center's opening was an article about a large drug confiscation just outside Salinger's city limits. With pictures of arrests, it was reported that this was part of a wider undercover operation in five states. It was part of an ongoing investigation, reportedly without the help of or any knowledge to local authorities. For months, the DEA had put agents in the area who had posed as independent truckers, exposing a large drug trafficking operation which intersected through Salinger. She wondered if Ben had seen the morning paper.

Chapter Thirty-Four

They set out that Saturday with a picnic packed in two light backpacks. Claire carried the one filled with the blanket, plastic wine glasses, plates, forks, and napkins. The food and wine were in Ben's thermal pack. Earlier in the morning, Claire had grilled portobello mushrooms and a few short skewers of marinated shrimp. They were having grilled shrimp along with sandwiches made from leftover pork tenderloin and the mushrooms. On the side, she prepared no-mayo coleslaw and finished with kitchen sink cookies for dessert.

It was a perfect day for a picnic. They put the bikes on the bike rack and drove fifteen miles west. This was going to be a leisurely day, and he was taking her somewhere they had never ridden before. It was more farmland, but every few miles in each direction, in every county, the terrain took on a different personality. He wanted her to see this area. If they liked the ride, they could easily leave from the house and ride this way, making it a thirty or forty mile cycling day. Today, though, it was about taking a new ride and stopping to picnic someplace unknown. Riding five miles out from the truck, they came upon a small apple orchard and stopped between the shady maples and the apple trees. While spreading out the blanket and setting up, both started sharing stories of family picnics. One of Claire's was of how she and her mother would have lunch looking out on the sunflowers. Then there were stories of family reunions. She had lots of stories about her brothers and friends in Chicago. Ben had plenty of stories growing up. He had so many cousins that between his brothers and cousins they had two baseball teams and got together every Sunday and played. No one could play sports at school because they had to be home to help on the farm every day, but Sundays they were the American League and National League all stars. From there they degenerated to stories of tailgating in college. They could always find a way to entertain each other.

Sipping on a chilled, light sauvignon blanc and enjoying the feast, they remained under the trees, affectionately chatting for hours. Ben admitted, "I haven't laughed as much, just hung out as much, or loved being with anyone as much as this ever in my life."

Claire kissed him for that and went on to say, "I want my friends to meet you sooner than this winter. I want to invite them to the farm and let them see us together so they can get to know you."

"What are you thinking of doing?" he asked. Knowing how much they all meant to her. They were like family, and he wanted to be her family now, too. Propped up on the blanket, he offered to go to Palm Beach in the winters if she would come back to the farm in the summers. Her answer was finally yes! As much as she knew she was in love, she still had trepidation sometimes. Looking up at the bright sky a fleeting thought moved through her, *I'm scared. Help me.*

They talked and planned and decided who to invite and where everyone would stay. Out of town guests could come in Friday and leave Sunday after breakfast. She wanted David and Justin there. After all, David was responsible for her keeping a level head this summer. She also wanted the Harris' there and her good friends Bob and Sandra Brown. Now, to mix the old with the new, locally they would invite Mat and Charity, Liz and John, and of course Norma and Jeff. There would be fourteen of them for dinner on the Saturday night.

Packed up and back on their bikes, Ben said, "We'll go a little farther this way then turn around." It was five o'clock by then, and the sun was beginning its decent in the sky. It was a little hillier here so they pedaled slowly, taking their time as they got their momentum back. Up ahead was an S curve. Claire loved coming upon these twists and turns in the roads. Nowhere but in farm country could you ride elbows and fast straight-aways like here. As they made the S and came up over the crest of the hill, there expanding in the sunlight was an incredibly familiar sight! A field of sunflowers -- blazing in the sun!

The plants were at least seven feet tall, like she remembered them when they were way over her head. The green and brown and gold bathed in the sunlight. The field perked up as if to see her. It wasn't the same one, but this was the field. This was the field that she had carried with her all of her life; the special place that Claire, her mother, took her back to every summer. It was their sunflower garden where they would walk through the towering sun shines, as they called them, being careful not to break any. They would wander around the field, play hide and seek, and count their footsteps in every direction. More memories surfaced. Finally she could remember; she saw her mother's face clearly again, saw her beautiful smile, and the flowers dancing in the wind and sun. "Ben -- stop!" He looked back and saw the tears streaming down her face. Coming back around, he got off his bike and held her there for a long time. She tried to explain but he already understood the significance, saying. "Know that I love you." Here was her sign to which she already had the answer. She knew everything was right and she belonged here.

Next day she made the calls and everyone was free for dinner the first Saturday in October. Out of town guests were all able to come in on the Friday before. She was excited to be planning a party again. Ben's house was perfect for entertaining. It had a western feel, but more formal and very masculine. That was changing though as it was becoming more obvious she was living there, too. There were fresh flowers in all the rooms now, making it feel like home.

She knew her friends and Ben would have their love of art in common. As soon as you walked in the house, in the middle of the center front hallway, stood a heavy mahogany round claw-foot table displaying a Remington bronze. Against the wall was a settee upholstered in an Indian blanket with a Charles Russell original oil painting above it. There were three original bronzes displayed on the first floor. This included the one in the entry, as well as one in the living room. That room had plush sofas, ottomans that doubled as tables, and a couple of wing chairs, all upholstered in fine Texas soft cowhide leather. Off to the side, there also sat a Stickley table and four chairs that looked out on the back of the house with its two sets of French doors stepping out to a stone patio. The house had recessed lighting everywhere, except for the chandeliers. Two crystal chandeliers hung in the living room, another lit the dining room, and there was a fourth over the bed in the master bedroom. She had joked with him, telling him she felt as if she was on the set of the old TV show *Dallas*. During his career he had done a lot of business out west and in Texas, telling her they did things big in Texas.

The dining room had a traditional William and Mary English mahogany table and chairs, and the long sideboard against the wall displayed the other Remington. Behind the dining room was the kitchen which looked out to the patio through three more sets of French doors. Stepping through a portico leading off from the kitchen and living room was the master bedroom. The doors to Ben's office made it accessible from the bedroom or the living room. Upstairs there were four bedrooms, each with its own bathroom. The rooms still needed to be finished, and she planned to start adding the final touches. Ben had built the house nine years ago and never finished the upstairs.

The house sat on land where Ben's family had farmed. The offices, farming operations, and packing house were six miles away. The house was surrounded on three sides by trees and sat far enough from any crossroads it could only be seen from the back field. At the end of the patio and beyond the garden was a large pergola, set back as a border, decoratively dividing the house and the grounds from the farm. Ben admitted he had never used it, and so had allowed it to become overgrown with grass and vines. She knew it would be the perfect place for a harvest moon dinner party.

RECIPES

Italian Vinaigrette

Make the vinaigrette the day before and refrigerate. Wisk together ¾ of a cup of olive oil, 4 tablespoons of white wine vinegar, 1 tablespoon of sugar, 1 clove of minced garlic, the zest of one lemon, ½ teaspoon of pepper, and a ½ teaspoon of sea salt. Add to that, ½ teaspoon of dried oregano, ¼ teaspoon of dried thyme, ½ teaspoon of dried basil. Store vinaigrette in a jar. Makes about 1 cup. If you prefer use your favorite store bought Italian vinaigrette instead.

Grilled Portobello Mushrooms

Place 2 medium Portobello mushrooms in a re-sealable plastic bag, and pour ¼ cup of vinaigrette over the mushrooms. Marinate for 30 minutes. Grill the mushrooms for 10-12 minutes on each side, turning often.

Grilled Marinated Shrimp

Peel and devein ½ pound of medium shrimp, about 8. Put 2 shrimp on each skewer. In a re-sealable plastic bag, pour ¼ cup of Italian vinaigrette over the shrimp and marinate for 30 minutes. Grill the shrimp for 3 minutes on one side, and 2 minutes on the other. Or until done to your liking.

No-Mayo Coleslaw

½ pound of shredded cabbage, about 3 cups

A handful of parsley, chopped

½ cup of shredded carrot, 2 carrots

1/3 cup of Italian Vinaigrette

Toss all the ingredients together and serve. Serves 4

Grilled Herb Crusted Pork Tenderloin

1 pork tenderloin (1.2-1.5 pounds)   Olive oil to coat
1 clove of minced garlic
Rosemary, thyme, sweet paprika, cumin, oregano,
pepper, sea salt

On a large piece of waxed or parchment paper sprinkle the spices on the paper liberally. Layer the spices beginning with the rosemary, then thyme, sweet paprika, a sprinkle of cumin, oregano, pepper, and sea salt. Wash the tenderloin and coat well with olive oil and minced garlic. Roll the tenderloin in the spices and coat it all over and roll the paper around the meat and place it in re-sealable plastic bag. Let it marinate for at least 3 hours or overnight.

Prepare the grill and grill the tenderloin turning occasionally until done. Approximately 12+ minutes per side. The internal temperature will be 150 when done. Remove from grill and let rest for 5 minutes before slicing. Serves 2 with leftovers for sandwiches the next day.

Kitchen Sink Cookies

¾ cup oats

½ teaspoon baking soda

¼ teaspoon salt

1 ½ sticks of unsalted butter

1 cup granulated sugar

¾ cup chopped pecans

¾ cup sweetened flaked coconut

½ cup chopped or dried apricots

1 ½ cups all purpose flour

½ teaspoon baking powder

1 teaspoon cinnamon

½ cup brown sugar

1 large egg

6 oz of semi sweet chocolate chunks

½ cup cranberries or raisins

Preheat the oven to 375 degrees. With a hand held mixer cream together the butter and both sugars. Add the egg. Stir in the flour, oatmeal, salt, cinnamon, baking powder and baking soda. Blend together well. Then stir in the pecans, chocolate chips, coconut, cranberries and dried apricots. Place tablespoonfuls of dough 2 inches apart on your prepared cookie sheet. Bake for 12 minutes or until golden brown. Makes about 30 cookies.

Chapter Thirty-Five

*B*en had a surprise for Claire, an invitation to a party given by Bill and Yvonne. The Klaussens were back in town and having one of their signature dinner parties.

Bill was happy to contribute to the success of the town. He and Ben had been friends their whole lives, so when one came to the other with a request or a proposition, the other always listened. This weekend Claire would meet the mystery donors.

Bill left Salinger after high school for college. Right after graduation he headed straight to New York. Through his father's long-standing relationships with every grower in the Midwest, Bill set up a hothouse vegetable wholesale company that defied anyone's expectations. He started his business at the perfect time, during the early eighties. While he timed his entry into the New York marketplace brilliantly, he was equally savvy in knowing when to get out. He sold the business to a private equity firm and became a very wealthy man. He made his key employees rich that day, too, showing his gratitude to all of them for their integrity and loyalty.

While in his New York base of operations, his primary clients had been the large chain grocers. He also had as clients some surviving mom and pop stores, the growing organic grocery markets, and the gourmet grocers throughout New York State, Connecticut, and northern and central New Jersey. Where he really made inroads, and developed an exceptional reputation, was in the boutique business with individual chefs and restaurateurs whose establishments became landmarks. Bill had a taste for the finest and always endeavored to find the absolute best in fresh and organic herbs and produce for clients like The Four Seasons, The Plaza, and The St. Regis. His little black book was filled with the private numbers of the most celebrated chefs throughout the country. He consulted for and provided financing to greenhouse operations throughout the Midwest, creating an annual bounty of whatever chefs desired.

After selling his business, one of the greenhouse farms he had done business with came up for sale. It happened to be twenty-six miles outside of Salinger. Bill and Yvonne bought the property and kept the farm running year round. They came back from time to time and threw dinner parties the likes of nothing Claire had ever before experienced. Palm Beach could learn from Bill and Yvonne. They called the property Greenwich Farm and invited chefs to come, cook, and share in the fun. Bill paid them to come and hired whatever staff they required. The menu was chef's choice. They created carte blanche seasonal dinners and had the run of the greenhouses for the best produce in house. Bill and Yvonne invited their friends from all over the country. The price of admission was to bring two bottles of your best wine. Bill invited Ben and Claire to this particular dinner and told them they could bring friends.

The festivities began at 6 p.m. so everyone could arrive before dark. Just a half mile from the main road, they drove in past three large, impressive greenhouses. There were small fields, or very large planting beds, all around the greenhouses. The local college used the farm as their specialty horticulture facility. In a trust, Bill and Yvonne had donated this to the school.

The main house was set back a mile and half from the farm and looked like a Tuscan stone villa with a long, circular gravel driveway. There were still late season remnants where the rose garden had bloomed at one end of the house and spilled onto the dining room patio. Fall wildflowers now blanketed the green grass.

The interior was furnished as a Tuscan home, simple yet elegant. Across the back of the house were the dining room and open kitchen. The commercial kitchen was state-of-the-art and had been designed by Chef Paul LeClerq, owner of The Grange, in New York City. The dining room was a gracious, open space with a grand stone fireplace at one end and opened to the kitchen on the other. The dining table sat twenty-four and the house slept the same. There was room for everyone. Most of the guests flew in for these dinners. Those who were close enough to drive were encouraged to stay, as well. It was assumed everyone was spending the night.

Claire was not supposed to know about the surprise dinner invitation. Ben just told her to dress up and bring an overnight bag with a casual change of clothes for the morning. He invited Mat and Charity but must have forgotten to tell Mat it was a surprise. Charity called Claire to find out what she was wearing and let the surprise out.

That weekend was Ben's fifty-eighth birthday. Claire thought of several things she wanted to do to celebrate, but every plan she started to put in place frustratingly fell through. He was insistent he would not travel far due to the harvest schedule and nothing she tried to plan worked out. Now she knew the real reason Ben was so resistant to her plans for this weekend.

An even better idea came to her. She called Greenwich Farm and told the secretary it was a guest's birthday. Could dessert include a birthday cake for Ben Donohue? That was all she needed to do. What an incredible menu! What an amazing party! Claire acted surprised, but at the end of the night the real surprise came when the decadent cake was brought out and everyone sang *Happy Birthday* and toasted Ben.

Chapter Thirty-Six

*T*hey were together every day now. Claire had grown so independent over the past few years she questioned if she could ever commit again. Ben had also questioned his own ability to recommit, having had a string of failed relationships in the past. Now he felt not only renewed, but important and wise and appreciated every minute he was with her. He felt a strong need to take care of her, yet there was nothing needy about her. He felt her passion and glow and simply wanted to be a part of her life.

What this summer brought was a realization there was another level to relationships that they had not known before. They brought to each other their strengths but also came with their weaknesses. The polarity of their equality and vulnerability charmed each one about the other. He often joked with her and told her she needed a strong man, one who could handle a strong woman like her.

Claire's point of view and near innocence in this new environment both intrigued and aroused him. They could both come together in child-like wonder at times, feeling safe and not judged by the other. There was a feeling of complete acceptance

Ben had never experienced before. They were exciting and stimulating to one another. And they made each other laugh.

He made a decision this woman was important to his life, hoping he had learned from his past mistakes. Claire, too, had a lifetime of old conditioning behind her. They discussed how they had their faults. Both came with past judgments, fears, attitudes, and with old beliefs about love that were passed down from their families, and ones they had made up themselves along the way. Now they knew it was time to let go of old habits. It was time to be new and all in -- time to write their own rules. This did not feel in any way like a compromise – they were creating a game plan.

Tonight the moonlight illumined Ben's heart and she glimpsed again into his soul, like he sometimes unwittingly allowed during these past few months together. Tonight he sensed she saw more than skin deep, and it was tender and passionate. As they looked in each other's eyes, she thought, *This is what I've longed for, it feels so good to finally say it again.* Claire whispered, "I'm so happy Ben."

Acknowledging this truth, he said, "I haven't felt this way before. I want to experience the love I have to give."

When he took her in his arms she felt safe and cherished. And they were both instantly relaxed and at peace. He was a powerful man, both in vocation and physically, and showing strength came naturally. But to exhibit vulnerability did not come so naturally at first. In her arms it eventually did. This kind of love had eluded both of them before. Here they found solace and a renewed youth and playfulness. She often caught herself singing the old song: *When a Man Loves a Woman.*

She awoke the next morning to the sound of rain hitting the window. Getting up to close it, she reflected back on the night before. A breeze brushed her arm and she raised her arm to her face, and held it there, still smelling him on her warm soft skin. Seeing him stir Claire walked over to the bed, bent down and gave him a kiss; then quietly she left the room. It was her turn to make Sunday morning breakfast.

It was going to be a lazy day. Sitting over breakfast, they looked out to see it was very grey, windy, and the rain was coming down much harder now. Max snoozed, curled up comfortably on his dog bed. It was his day off from chasing small animals all over the yard. Claire pulled her chair around, up to Ben's, facing him. "Have you ever made the trip from your head to your heart?" she asked.

Looking up from the morning paper, "I don't know what you're talking about," was his reply.

She scooted her chair in to get closer, put her hand in the center of his chest, and said, "Bring your mind down behind my hand." She paused to let him try and move his mind down, toward his heart. "If it's easier, put your own hand up to your chest, and hold it there." He put down the paper; she took his hand and moved it up to the center of his chest, and held it there with him. "Can you make yourself move your mind down? As you do that, can you feel a warmth, behind your hand?" They rested their hands there while he tried to do it.

"What do you mean?" he asked, puzzled.

She moved her hand away. "Keep your hand on your chest and let it get your mind's attention. Take your mind down through your body to where your hand is." With her hand on her chest she was doing it as well.

"OK, I'm doing it, now what?"

"Do it some more. Now move your hand away. Can you keep your mind down in your chest, in your heart?"

"It's not so easy," he said.

"Hand to your chest -- hand on your heart -- move down to your heart again. Do you feel that?"

"Yeah, it's warm." He responded.

"You're such a good student, and you say all the right things," Easing forward, she kissed him. Bringing his attention back she said, "Now do it again, and this time, bring your mind along." They paused as he journeyed his listening, from his head, those eighteen inches down to his heart. "Listen to me speaking to you -- from your heart. Keep your hand there if it helps. Listen with your heart. Now that you've been down to your heart, and know the way there, how does that feel?"

"Warm, different," was all he said.

"Can you make the space that feels warm bigger than your hand?"

There was a long pause. "Yeah, I'm doing it," Ben said.

"You're opening your heart -- bigger. Listening from our hearts we hear what's said differently. It's listening from a loving place, from a non-judging place. Our hearts don't think, instead, they recognize and understand intuitively. Go back up to your head and listen to me." She talked about their day. "Now drop down, listen from your heart as I speak to you again." He acknowledged a distinction. "It's not always easy but we can remind each other at times to step down to our hearts when we listen."

Chapter Thirty-Seven

*B*en was happy, the final crop had come in as planned. It was nearly the end of September and he was harvesting onions. This summer had flown by and it had been significant in every way. Before she left Palm Beach in the spring, her friends all teased she was crawling under a rock. Her response now was she took the rock and created a Michelangelo.

Today they were taking one of their favorite rides, a twenty-six mile route in a southeasterly direction with no backtracking. They rode up a slow, long hill for the first three miles. That got them set and warmed up. Turning right onto Plymouth Road, they rode into the wind on an eight-mile straight away. There were several Amish farms in this area and all were immaculate. Now their vegetable and flower gardens were overflowing with squashes, and pumpkins were spreading throughout the yards. The perennial flower beds, which had been supplying kitchen tables with fresh cut flowers all summer long, were all trimmed back and mums replaced the colorful blooms for fall. They rode past Amish buggies and passed the little two-room schoolhouse which sat at the fork in the road.

Looking out over the fields, the corn stalks were nearly translucent as they stood drying in the fall sun, awaiting combines to come through. Farmers in their combines were out from early morning until dark, roaring through fields harvesting corn for cattle feed and ethanol plants. A few weeks earlier Claire watched as sweet corn was being harvested. Workers in the fields, hand-picked three thousand crates of corn a day. Ben explained the flavor of corn depended on weather conditions. "If it rains within a week of harvest time, the flavor of the corn isn't nearly as sweet. Corn's sweetness also depends on the temperatures dipping down at night." He remarked this had been a good harvest year because the days were hot and the nights had been cool.

Everything was turning to gold. The tips of the leaves on the trees were beginning to change into their fall foliage colors. Looking around, the soybean fields had changed from their green-blue brilliance to the now familiar dry, burnished golden color. She reflected how beautiful plants looked as they stood dying, likening it to an opera -- where the heroine let out her most extraordinary range of voice and motion, exclaiming the end! So too, in their own way, did the trees and plants give one last peak performance before the combines crashed through and left only the dust to settle for days as quiet was restored. Deciding not to share this metaphor with Ben, smiling, she knew she had gone too far again.

Once they crossed Section Line Road, the next six miles took them past Bell's sheep farm and Mr. Haupt the egg man's place. The eggs tasted so much better fresh from their chicken coup than from the store. This part of the ride was fast, and they could easily go sixteen to eighteen miles per hour on the hybrids. Most days they did not pass even one car on this stretch. Around the turn, they stopped in the little gully to take a drink under the shady canopy where the leaves had already turned scarlet red.

The last nine miles were flat, easy roads past the Adam's farm, where earlier in the summer they had stopped to help. Riding side by side, they had talked a lot this summer. Pedaling along was not a solitary sport at all. It was a great place to communicate. Yes, Claire had learned many farm facts, but they had also expressed their feelings. They conveyed what they thought about life and shared how their lives were changing now. She referred to the outside air as truth serum, because they talked about intimate things where it sometimes takes a distraction to obtain a straight answer. They agreed they would communicate whatever was on their mind. And as with all intense exercise, as their testosterone levels went up, they teased one another. Claire asked, "How do you feel?"

"Alive! Young! Happy!" he called out. "And you?"

"Happy! Sexy! Loved!" Then she asked, "What else?"

"Claire, you give me peace of mind. I feel all man with you, and around you, girl, I'm still learning!"

"I love you Ben!" They could see a car behind them a short distance away, and Ben rode up ahead of her. As they returned home up the driveway, they saw hawks soaring and the strange-looking turkey vultures eating in the fields. Adjacent to the birds was the doe with her growing fawn, whose spots had completely vanished.

They got cleaned up, he opened a bottle of pinot noir, and they sat in the kitchen. It was too cold to sit outside anymore. She had made a delicious, creamy squash soup in the morning, which was perfect after a chilly ride. There was leftover steak from the night before. She spread crusty whole-grain bread with brie and mounded slices of cold, rare filet on top, finishing it off with grainy Dijon mustard. There was an arugula salad on the side and dark chocolate for dessert.

RECIPES

Squash Soup

4 medium acorn squash	8 slices of bacon, crisply broiled
3 tablespoons olive oil	1 medium onion, peeled and chopped
2 stalks of celery, with leaves, chopped	2 cloves of garlic
2" piece of ginger, peeled and chopped	½ teaspoon cumin
1 teaspoon sweet paprika	½ teaspoon powdered sage
1 scant teaspoon pepper	2 large bay leaves
¼ teaspoon cayenne pepper	8 cups chicken stock
Salt to taste	

½ cup half & half

Cut squash in halves and place in a pan sitting in 1½ inches of water. Bake at 375 for 40 minutes or until soft. Remove from oven and keep warm with a clean dishcloth over them. In your soup terrine, sauté in oil, the onion, minced garlic, celery, and ginger. Throw away the seeds and scoop the squash out of the shells and add to the onions. Stir and add in the cumin, paprika, sage, and pepper. Blend well and sauté for a couple of minutes more. Add the chicken stock and bay leaves. Boil on medium heat for 1 hour. Turn off the stove and let the soup rest for a few minutes. Remove the bay leaves. Puree the soup. Add the cayenne, and crumble in the bacon. Add salt if necessary. Add the half and half. Blend well.

Chapter Thirty-Eight

*T*he Center was up and operational. Charity had acquainted herself quickly with the workings of the business side, as she was the interface with the public school system as well as the community. Claire had already taken the private project in Nashville, Tennessee. She was also working with the Cuyahoga County School Board in the Cleveland-area schools. Salinger's "Off-Campus Children's Center" was a working model which had caught the interest of other Ohio-area schools, and for that Claire had Norma to thank.

The weather was beautiful. Crisp autumn sights and smells were all around. Trees were flushed in their glorious orange and crimson, and only about a week away from showing off their peak colors. The timing was perfect, as this was finally the week Claire's friends would arrive. Leading up to the weekend, she had been giving Ben background information about everyone who was coming, starting with David. "You'll finally meet David. David and Justin are driving down from Chicago and will turn around and drive back on Sunday. Justin splits his time equally between Chicago and Palm Beach, David stays in Chicago a little more. They actually met up north. Justin has an art gallery on the Near North

Side of Chicago and another in Palm Beach. David works, as you know, in the electronics business. He owns a large distribution company, which his father started. David has said, once his mother overcame the guilt and shame she perceived about having a gay son, she pestered his father to bring him into the business. She explained it would set the highest of examples for their friends. Too, it would improve the father-son relationship, since any relationship would have been an improvement over what they had until then. His father succumbed to the pressures from his mother and David began working with him. That was twenty years ago. His business and law background brought a fresh perspective, and his style was very different from his father's. They became a great team and built a highly successful company." Claire went on, saying, "David and Justin met about thirteen years ago, and moved in together soon afterwards. At the time, Justin hadn't come out yet and dreaded visiting home. It took three years, a breakup, and therapy before he introduced David to his family as his partner. David often laughs saying, 'Ultimately, the redeeming quality to this relationship for both of our mothers was that we each had brought home another good Jewish boy'."

Claire loved them both and they had become a great threesome over the years. "Then they introduced me to Sandra and Bob, who are serious art collectors. They're from New York, but spend most of their time, when not traveling, in Florida. That's also how Justin and David came to know Pat and Stephen Harris, originally as art collectors. Pat and Stephen are also from Chicago and we've been friends for a long time. Our children grew up together." Claire explained, "You know how after a divorce people unfortunately feel a need to choose sides -- Pat and Stephen chose me." Throughout the past twelve years in Palm Beach, the friends all said as soon as she was serious about someone they had to meet him and give their blessings on the union. *Thank goodness no one had died waiting,* Claire mused.

Sandra and Bob flew up from Palm Beach and were driving in from the Columbus airport; Pat and Stephen drove down from Chicago. They would continue on to Palm Beach, returning south only a couple of weeks earlier than usual this year. Having this weekend trip in Ohio broke up the first part of their trip back, and they always stopped in Atlanta, Georgia, to visit their older daughter and her family for a few days. Their two youngest had grown up friends with Claire's children.

They all arrived at about the same time on Friday, causing a huge commotion in the entry. With each new arrival the excitement, hugging, laughter, and talking over one another got louder, more effuse, and kept repeating. "Hey, everybody!" Claire called for everyone's attention, "I want you to meet Ben." The whole swarm moved about two feet over and did the very same to him; introducing themselves, shaking hands, giving him pats, and hugging him as if they had all been long time friends. Shaking hands and laughing Ben said to David, "We did it. She's back. It's good to finally meet you."

Once things settled down, Claire showed everyone to their rooms so they could take their bags upstairs and freshen up. Soon after, they all came back down and noticed the dining room table was already set for dinner. The house smelled deliriously good. The savory aromas coming from the kitchen beckoned everyone. They saw when they walked back to the kitchen there was a pot of veal stew simmering on the stove, with fresh herbs already chopped sitting on the counter, waiting to go in during the last few minutes of cooking. The pasta, which Claire bought in Columbus when she went shopping for the weekend, was homemade and would just take minutes to prepare. There was also a crisp romaine salad waiting for starters. Pat walked over to the stove, lifted the lid on the stew and gave it a stir just so she could enjoy the smell close up. Everyone commented, "What have you done to our Claire, she doesn't cook. Next we'll see her barefoot and pregnant in the kitchen." Claire assured them all it was impossible, but thanked them for their compliments. While congregating in the kitchen, they had hors d'oeuvres and glasses of champagne to celebrate coming together and to toast the newest member of their tribe. Then they all wanted a tour of the house, so Ben obliged, while Claire finished preparing dinner.

Afterward, everyone was seated. Calling dinner delicious was an understatement. After several toasts went around the table, they all launched into telling stories about their summer adventures. They heard the details about Bob and Sandra's trip to Italy; some of Claire's adventures at the farm, especially how she and Ben met; and the state of Justin's art business. They talked about what a hot summer it had been in Chicago and who the artists were Justin planned to exhibit this winter season in the southern gallery. Everyone embraced Ben. Every discussion was set up so he felt included and knew the time lines and people. She could see he was fitting right in. Whenever this group got together, there was more information shared than necessary.

The last time they were all together was in Palm Beach at Sandra and Bob's before everyone disbanded for the summer. At the time, they made a pact that from then on they would get together every summer at someone's home, never waiting again until they all returned south in the fall.

During all the conversation, it turned out no one had ever been to a farm before – no surprise really, so Ben planned a field trip. Whoever wanted to could follow him over to the farm in the morning. His foreman Jose would be there to meet them. He would give a tour to whoever wanted one. Or if someone wanted to see the last of the harvesting taking place, or ride in a combine, they could do that, too. If anyone wanted to drive a tractor, that could be arranged as well. Claire explained, "Sorry this isn't a dairy farm, so no one gets to milk a cow." She added it was regrettably the one thing she had not done this summer.

Saturday everyone rushed to get through breakfast, wanting to get over to the farm by 9 a.m. Charity insisted she was in charge of all desserts and muffins for the weekend, so early in the morning she came for coffee and brought over two dozen carrot-walnut and zucchini muffins.

In the afternoon, Claire let them know they were on their own or could cycle through the country with Ben. After hearing Claire's stories all summer long, Justin and David got on the hybrids, and Stephen took a road bike. Sandra and Bob went into town to explore. Pat stayed behind to help Claire, and Charity was on her way over to Mrs. Steiner's to pick up three homemade pies: pumpkin, cherry, and apple.

Two of the workers from the farm who helped around the house came over and set up the furniture inside the pergola. They had worked much of the last week clearing away the weeds and cutting down the tall grass. They cut back the dead vines. The grapes were still ripe and tumbled over the outer trellises. The vines had filled in nicely all summer long, giving the structure an undercover, sheltered feeling. Inside they set up fourteen chairs and brought down two long tables, butting them together end to end. The structure sat about forty feet from the house and the same stone that made up the patio also led out with a walkway through the lawn and garden to the twenty-five foot long covered dining area, all set up for the evening.

Pat and Claire set the table, brought out the silver candelabras, and lined votives down the center of the table. Claire did not want flowers obstructing anyone's view, so instead they scattered brightly colored leaves, small pumpkins, and squash around the place settings. Early in the morning Claire had begun cooking, preparing what she needed to so most of the dishes could bake later in the ovens. She hired the only caterer in town to make the hors d'oeuvres, serve, and cleanup. Patty and Sue were the owners and were stopping off at the butcher in Somerset to pick up the meat on their way over to the house. Mr. Gallagher was preparing two lamb loins. Claire had given him explicit instructions how to grill these, and he promised he would do exactly as she requested. The caterers would be at the house at five. They already knew what to do when they arrived and would take over all the prep from there.

Around four that afternoon the friends converged again and began telling their stories. The cyclists had taken an easy back roads ride that wound around the farm and went through the little town of Redding, stopping for sodas and sandwiches at Bert's Bar.

They each went to get ready, and everyone began coming down as others arrived just before six. Ben introduced Liz and John, and Norma and Jeff, to everyone. Charity and Mat arrived a few minutes later. The pies were still warm when they carried them into the kitchen.

The weather had been Claire's only concern, but it did not disappoint as Indian summer came across the area during that whole week, making it a mild autumn night. They all went out on the patio to have hors d'oeuvres and cocktails while the sun set and the moon came out. It was a big, bright harvest moon that night. As it hung low in the sky, it lit the path so they could see while making their way down to dinner.

The table was beautifully set and the candles shimmered in the gentle breeze, illuminating the night. As each person walked under the vine canopy to find their place, their eyes lit up and enchanted expressions showed excitement at seeing the romantic atmosphere of the long, candlelit, inviting table that sprawled before them. Claire put a name by each place setting so there would be a little mingling in the group, but friends would still be close by and could mix freely. The first course was served; it was asparagus, pancetta, and leeks sautéed and served over crisped polenta. The toasting got started with Ben welcoming everyone. He looked genuinely taken by the atmosphere she had created and told her so, with another toast.

Claire, Liz, and Pat picked up the dishes when they were all finished, and went back up to the house to help with bringing down the main course. On the way up, Pat squeezed Claire's hand and said "Claire, he's wonderful!" and Liz agreed. Patty and Sue were just about finished plating the main course, then the five of them carried the dishes down. In front of each person sat a plate brimming with a delectable feast of local delicacies. Claire stood up to make a toast and describe dinner. There was lamb grilled to perfection. She smiled, thrilled with Mr. Gallagher. The sides were roasted fingerling rosemary potatoes, which she wanted them to know had come out of the rear-quarter field. There was a root vegetable gratin, fresh green beans finished in the oven, and roasted red peppers. The sweet shallot glaze for the lamb was a sensual ruby red and was passed around. And for the purists around the table, there was mint jelly. The table was set with wonderful pinots and French Burgundy wines. Everyone imbibed savoring the flavors and aromas; delighted moans and compliments kept rising.

Everyone was busy talking and laughing. Conversations went back and forth across the table as everyone began catching up and others found things in common. Bob and Liz knew people in common in Washington. Justin and Ben talked about the Remington's and the Western art in the house. As the night sky seemed to get brighter, the mood became more pleasured and everyone was happy to be together. Claire looked around and saw Mat holding Charity's hand. And she loved the way Norma and Jeff were having such a good time with Liz and John; she always loved hearing Norma's giggle. Pat looked beautiful tonight, and she and Stephen quietly flirted as they talked to David and Justin. Claire turned back to Ben and reached over for his hand. He loved the way her small hand fit in his, and he kissed it. Then David looked up and commented on the beautiful Chuppah in which they were having dinner. Ben was confused as he did not know the word. Bob and Sandra both chimed in that this was the perfect setting for a wedding and didn't they all agree! That picked up the volume and everyone chided Ben and Claire. It was too soon to kiss and tell.

After the table was cleared, coffee and dessert were brought down -- the pies with several pints of ice cream. Dessert was served family style and was passed around the table, so everyone could help themselves. Everyone had so much more to say; dessert and the conversations just kept on going.

Earlier, Ben was concerned it might cool down later in the evening. The trellises kept the wind out and the burning candles kept everyone warm while they ate, but now it was getting chilly. He had prepared the fire pit earlier in the day, just in case, and now he had a fire blazing. The whole party moved over to the campfire. He brought out some blankets and extra jackets for everyone. City boy Bob accidentally caught his jacket on fire! They all rushed to wrap him in a blanket while they tackled him to the ground to put out the fire. Knowing he was safe, they all burst out laughing, even mortified Sandra. She had not worried for his safety, as she knew he was in good boy scout hands, but rather that her husband tripped and nearly went up in flames. Even she joined in laughing now. There was a big pot of coffee on the grate and a cooler still brimming with wine. How anyone could have room left after dinner was questionable, but just in case, there were plenty of sticks, marshmallows, shortbreads, and chocolate waiting for later. Ben saw to that. They all sat around snuggling in the crisp fall air, laughing, and now the men started telling ghost stories they remembered from childhood. The women squealed, giggled, and sat hiding their faces completely grossed out, while the guys encouraged one another to tell more.

Later the mood changed as everyone was feeling content. They began singing campfire songs -- like the Rolling Stones, the Beatles, and Van Morrisson. Claire took out her cell phone and called up to the house. When Patty and Sue were finished cleaning up they could let themselves out, but first turn up the music. The women all looked beautiful tonight, and the men were charming and so good looking. Many got up, and they began to dance, and danced late into the night. No one noticed the fire had turned to embers. Ben tapped on Stephen's shoulder, who in turn tapped on Mat's. As the moon lit the path they all walked back to the house. It was one of those great nights you never forget sharing pleasure and making memories.

RECIPES

Veal Stew

3.5-4 pounds of veal for stew	1 large sweet onion, diced
Vegetable or Canola oil	2 cloves of garlic, pressed
1 red pepper seeded and diced	2 tablespoons flour
2 tablespoons of sweet paprika	1 teaspoon pepper
3-4 cups chicken stock	2 tablespoons tomato paste
6 carrots cleaned and chopped in ½ inch pieces	
1 scant teaspoon apple cider vinegar	Salt to taste
½ cup of fresh parsley	¼ cup of fresh thyme

In a heavy saucepan with enough oil in the bottom sauté the onion until wilted, add the red pepper and garlic. Continue sautéing a few minutes more. Now add the veal, salt lightly, and sauté on medium high heat turning often until the meat is browned. Reduce heat and add the flour and paprika. Blend well, scraping the bottom, so the flour does not burn. Add 2 cups of chicken stock and continue scraping the sides and bottom. Bring to a boil and add the tomato paste. Cook for 5 minutes then add the additional stock and carrots. Simmer for 1.5 hours more. During cooking if the stew seems thick add additional chicken stock. You want it to be more like a dense broth than thick like a traditional stew. Add the cider vinegar and check seasoning. Add the herbs and let the stew rest for about 30 minutes. Just before serving heat through. Serve over fettucini or any other wide noodles. Serves 8.

Asparagus, Pancetta, and Leek Sauté over Crisped Polenta

Make the polenta in the morning or at least several hours ahead so it is cold and firm when you slice it. You can prepare it according to cornmeal package directions or like the recipe below.

Crisped Polenta

2 cups of chicken stock or water   1 cup ground cornmeal
¼ cup milk   Olive oil
Salt and pepper to taste

Prepare an 8x8 pan with a little olive oil. In a medium saucepan bring water or stock to a boil. Wisk the cornmeal constantly as you add it to the liquid. Turn the heat on low and continue wisking as it cooks for another minute. You want the polenta to be thick and smooth. Wisk in the milk and season with salt and pepper. Remove from heat and pour into the prepared pan. Spread the polenta evenly in the pan. Cover and refrigerate.

Cut the polenta in any shape you'd like. For now cut into 2x3 inch bars. Use enough olive oil in your pan to lightly fry the polenta bars. Fry each side to a golden brown.

Asparagus, Pancetta and Leek sauté

¼ pound of pancetta or 6 strips of bacon, chopped	1 pound of asparagus
3 leeks	A healthy sprinkling of pepper
½ cup white wine	Shaved parmesan cheese

Wash and trim the asparagus. Cut in 3 inch sections. Place in boiling water and cook for 3 minutes. Drain water and place asparagus in ice water to stay crisp and bright green. Keeping about 2 inches of the green bottoms wash and trim the leeks. Cut them vertically down the center. Wash and clean well. Now chop the leeks. In a heavy skillet brown the pancetta or bacon. Remove pancetta. Using the same skillet pour the grease out and brown the leeks in the remaining coating left in the skillet. Pour in the wine and deglaze the pan to make a sauce. Boil for 5 minutes. Return the asparagus and pancetta back to the skillet. Cook for another few minutes until heated through. Spoon over crisped polenta and top with parmesan cheese. Serves 8.

Grilled Lamb

6 pound leg of lamb per 8 people. Have the leg boned, butterflied, and trimmed of fat and connective tissue.

1 tablespoon sea salt	½ cup fresh mint leaves
1 cup of fresh Italian parsley	½ cup fresh rosemary
8 cloves of garlic	
2 tablespoons cumin	
1 tablespoon curry powder	1 tablespoon black pepper

1 teaspoon cayenne pepper, optional, depending on how much heat you like

2/3 cup olive oil

Place lamb in a big enough pan or cookie sheet and salt well. Use a food processor and combine the remaining ingredients. You may have to scrape the sides to blend well. Spread the mixture over both sides of the lamb. Cover the lamb and refrigerate overnight. Grill lamb for 15 minutes per side for medium rare. Adjust for your taste. Let meat rest when done. Slice the meat across the grain for a more tender cut.

Sweet Shallot Glaze

6 shallots

½ teaspoon pepper

½ cup plus of chicken stock

¼ cup of plum or currant jelly

3 tablespoons of butter

A sprinkling of flour

¼ cup of white wine

Peel and chop the shallots. Sauté them in the butter for 10-12 minutes or until soft. Sprinkle flour to coat the shallots. Add the chicken stock. Stir well, on high heat. Add the white wine and let boil off for 5 minutes. If it seems too thick add a little more chicken stock. Remove from heat. Warm the jelly, strain and pour into the sauce. Serve with the lamb.

Roasted Fingerling Rosemary Potatoes

2 pounds of fingerling or small   Sea salt
red potatoes

1/3 cup olive oil   Fresh or dried rosemary

Sweet paprika

In an oblong baking pan toss the potatoes with the oil, salt
and a liberal amount of rosemary and paprika. Bake for 25
minutes then turn the potatoes. Let them brown evenly. Bake
an additional 20 minutes.

Roasted Red Peppers

4-5 red bell peppers   2 cloves of garlic
½ cup olive oil   3 - 4 tablespoons of balsamic vinegar
Salt and pepper

Grill or place the peppers under the broiler. Turn frequently until the outside is well charred, being careful not to puncture them. When they are finished carefully place them in a salad bowl. Cover the bowl with a clean dishcloth and allow them to rest for 30 minutes or more. Return to the peppers -- puncture them and allow the juice to collect in the bottom of the bowl. Remove the outer skins, tops and seeds. They will peel easily if the bowl was covered. Add olive oil, garlic put through a press, and vinegar. Season with salt and pepper to taste. They can be made the day before. Dip bread in the oil mixture. Serves 8.

S'mores

Roast marshmallows over a fire, when they are done to your liking immediately, but careful not to burn yourself, put them between 2 graham crackers or shortbreads with a piece of chocolate in between.

Chapter Thirty-Nine

*S*unday morning coffee was ready as they came down to the kitchen one by one. Calls started coming in after nine o'clock that morning; Liz called to thank Claire, letting her know they had gotten home safely. Same came from Charity and soon after, Norma. The muffins, fruit, and yogurt were waiting on the table. The eight of them sat and talked about the night before, their departures, and best ways to go. They all wanted to make the visit last as long as they could.

By eleven, everyone was packed and ready to go. They all had a long drive ahead of them and stood outside in the driveway, giving one another one last hug and letting everyone know their scheduled returns to Palm Beach. Claire looked up at Ben saying, "We'll be there soon, around November first." The last car was seen leaving down the driveway as Claire and Ben turned to walk back into the house. The cold air was coming in and a light drizzle was just beginning to come down. Ben put his arm around her, holding her tight and keeping her warm and close. As they walked back into the house, he said, "Next May, when we're both back here, I want to plant a large sunflower field behind the house, like the one we saw the day of our picnic."

With her heart wide open she looked in his eyes and said, "It's so good to be home."

BOOK GROUP QUESTIONS AND DISCUSSION TOPICS

1. The Law of Attraction states: first *Ask for what you want* – be clear on your request; then *Believe* that the request or desire is already being fulfilled; then *Receive* the outcome -- What did Norma, Claire, Charity, and Ben each *Ask* for? How were their desires fulfilled? Give an example of the Law of Attraction in your life.

2. The farmland is as much a character in the book as the people. For example soil (earth) and water are basic resources in farm country. The metaphysical metaphor for earth and water are the body and emotions. What are the similarities between the land and characters?

3. What does Claire's mother represent in the book?

4. What do you think of Charity? How did she become friends with Claire? She and Claire are so different what was the attraction?

5. What does Charity rediscover or in fact recover?

6. What occurred in chapter 24 and how does it lead to what happens in the next chapter? Why did Claire choose to be a strong advocate for children?

7. Letting go is a theme that weaves throughout the book. Why is it so important? How many times does it come up and in what ways do the characters let go?

8. Are Ben and Claire really that much different? What is it about Ben you most like or dislike?

9. In Chapter 36 what are the ways Claire and Ben plan to make their relationship work.

10. The recipes are an allegory for what is taking place throughout the book. Explain this, and how is Charity's reaction to the foods Claire prepares representative of what she is experiencing? How are Claire's recipes symbolic of her own life?

11. What do the sunflowers signify to Claire?

12. Take the journey from your head to your heart.

ACKNOWLEDGMENTS

My deep love and appreciation goes to my daughters, friends, and my master mind group.

You are always there supporting me in every way.

Also I want to acknowledge Randy Testa, Bob Stouffer, and my editor Laura Tichy-Smith.

And thank you to Richard Rogers and all my teachers.

ABOUT THE AUTHOR

Loving being in nature and cycling, an extended visit to Ohio farm country inspired this debut novel, *25,000 SEEDS*.

Also the author of *Being Simply Beautiful*. Helen Noble is the founder and CEO of a natural cosmetics company and lives in Naples Florida.

www.25000seeds.com

Made in the USA
Lexington, KY
21 November 2013